Miss Mary-Kate Martin's GUIDE TO MONSTERS

The Wrath of the Woolington Wyrm

KAREN FOXLEE

Illustrated by Freda Chiu

PUSHKIN CHILDREN'S

Pushkin Press
Somerset House, Strand
London WC2R 1LA

The Wrath of the Woolington Wyrm was first published by
Allen & Unwin, Australia, 2022

First published by Pushkin Press in 2023

1 3 5 7 9 8 6 4 2

ISBN 13: 978-1-78269-413-7

Offset by Tetragon, London
Printed and bound by Clays Ltd, Elcograf S.p.A.

www.pushkinpress.com

For Alice May Foxlee.
KF

For my nephew, Jasper. May you
always be strong and soft.
FC

MAP OF WOOLINGTON WELL

TRAIN
STATION

HOOK &
WYRM INN

N

The earth trembled as the creature left its lair at night. It wound its way across the fields and slunk over the town bridge. It slithered across the churchyard and its skin shimmered as it slid past the windows of sleeping children. Its shadow raced along the stone walls by the light of the moon. It glided across the village green and then silently through the narrow cobblestoned streets. It went past the pub and the tiny teashops, past the village library, searching. It had known the place for centuries. In the market square it stopped.

It let out a screech that was wild and full of rage.

That cry echoed down the laneways, through the thatched roof cottages, reverberated over the fields.

It was a noise that had not been heard for many years.

It is a common misconception that monster hunters need much equipment: rope, nets, stun guns, night-vision goggles, cages and lorries. It is important to note that none of these items are necessary.

P.K. Mayberry's Complete Guide to Monsters of the Northern Hemisphere

Miss Mary-Kate Martin chose from her lucky items collection carefully. First, she chose the lucky silver packet that contained the last seven pieces of gum that her father had left behind before he disappeared on Mount Shishapangma when she was five. She placed it carefully at the bottom of her suitcase.

She also chose the lucky novelty torch shaped like Big Ben and her lucky stress ball, which was a miniature world globe. It didn't seem nearly enough lucky things for a train trip to somewhere she'd never been, so she added her lucky international coin collection that contained thirty-three coins in a small glass jar.

'Make sure you pack sensible shoes,' her mother, Professor Martin, called from her bedroom.

Mary-Kate looked down at the red sparkly shoes she was wearing.

'Yes, Prof,' she said. Prof was what Mary-Kate called her mother.

Mary-Kate's dress and hair bow were black. Her shoes were red and so was her backpack. Both of them were sparkly. It was all perfectly coordinated, with exactly the right proportions of sparkle and colour. It made her feel good. If she changed the shoe colour it would mess things up. She'd be only twenty-five per cent sparkly. She'd begin to worry. She'd worry that by not wearing matching clothes something would happen. Something terrible. Like a train crash. Or an avalanche. Or an avalanche onto a train travelling through a mountain tunnel. Especially the train she was going to travel on that morning. Although she doubted there were any mountains or snow on the way to Woolington Well, she couldn't be one hundred per cent sure, so she packed her favourite lucky oversized handkerchief as well.

Many things set off these types of thoughts:

* Brown colouring-in pencils

* Beginnings and endings

* Facing backwards on trains

* Saying the wrong thing during small talk

* And sudden changes.

That morning had been filled with change.

'Archaeological digs require sensible shoes,' said Professor Martin, coming to stand at the door. She was wearing her sensible tan trousers, brown boots and brown utility jacket. Brown was a problem for Mary-Kate, but at least all the colours matched. 'Are you feeling anxious?'

She sat on Mary-Kate's bed and looked at the pile of lucky things in the suitcase.

'No,' lied Mary-Kate.

'I think it will be fun to have you along on a work trip with me. And exciting! I've heard it's a darling little village and you will have lots to explore.'

'What about my geography project? It's due on Wednesday,' said Mary-Kate, hopefully. Maybe she could stay at home alone. It was only two nights.

'You can do it on the train.' Professor Martin smiled.

'It's not that I don't want to go with you,' said Mary-Kate, picking up her lucky stress ball and giving it a forceful squish. 'It's just, well …'

'A bit out of the ordinary?'

Professor Martin was always catching trains and planes to faraway places for archaeological work. Mary-Kate had never been with her before.

'I'm used to staying with Granny,' Mary-Kate said apologetically.

'I know. But Granny is on one of her bus trips; you know how she loves them. So, it hasn't worked out this time.'

Besides her mother, Mary-Kate's granny was her favourite person in the world, even if she wore colourful mismatched clothes. Granny loved spicy international cuisine and when Professor Martin was away, she ordered takeaway and let Mary-Kate stay up late to watch the shopping channel, which Mary-Kate found soothing. They would go for long walks together around the park, side by side, comfortably silent.

Lately, though, Granny had discovered bus trips. She'd been to Scotland and then to Stonehenge, and now she was going in the Channel Tunnel to Paris. She seemed to be forever packing up her zebra-print suitcase with floral scarves and leopard-print tracksuits and heading out the front door.

Mary-Kate squished her globe stress ball again.

'It will be fun, Mary-Kate. A few days off school. I know it's been tricky for you there lately,' said Professor Martin kindly.

'Tricky' was not the word Mary-Kate would have used to describe how she'd been feeling at her school, Bartley Towers. If she used the H scale of how Horrid it had been there lately, she would be registering a triple H. Some days were one H days. Horrible. Others were double H days. Horrible and Horrendous. Lately they'd been triple H days. Horrible, Horrendous and Hideous.

La-la-la, she said to herself, because this sometimes helped to get rid of bad thoughts. She squeezed the globe stress ball extra hard.

'Why don't you pack some sensible clothes, Mary-Kate?' said Professor Martin, hopefully. 'And remember to pack your lucky stress ball too.'

Mary-Kate's mother went back to her own packing. Mary-Kate knew the Professor's hard-shell suitcase would contain nothing but sensible clothes in shades of brown. There would also be lots of digging tools, torches, brushes and special sprays. Professor Martin had been going away on archaeological digs for as long as Mary-Kate could remember and she'd watched her pack many times.

Mary-Kate looked wistfully at the lucky items she'd packed and added her second-favourite lucky oversized handkerchief as well. Into her backpack she placed her geography homework, her unused strawberry-scented notebook and unopened glitter pens, and her mobile phone. She placed her lucky stress ball on top. She'd need it on the train.

'Are you nearly ready?' called Professor Martin. 'The taxi will be here any minute.'

On the train, Mary-Kate was glad that her seat faced forwards. She tried not to think about the fact that she was going on a work trip with her mother to a place she didn't know. The only place they'd travelled to together was their annual holiday to the seaside. Each year they went to the exact same hotel with Granny and ate the exact same breakfasts and dinners, and played the exact same games of cards at night. Mary-Kate closed her eyes and wished that this was where they were going. Perhaps if she kept her eyes closed long enough that could actually happen? A whole season could pass, and she'd open her eyes and it would be summer and there would be Granny eating crisps and playing solitaire on her phone as familiar countryside whizzed past.

'Perhaps you could do your project?' suggested Professor Martin, who always knew when Mary-Kate was anxious.

'That might help,' said Mary-Kate, taking out her homework notebook and her pens.

Only it didn't.

It was the pens that were the trouble.

Twelve glitter pens in a plastic case, unopened.

Back in the safety of her bedroom with all her lucky things packed, she'd added the pens, thinking, *This is definitely the kind of day that I will be able to open my pens. Number 1: I will have no choice. I have no other pens packed. Number 2: Today feels like a pen packet-opening day.*

Here on the train, she held them in her lap unopened.

They looked so perfectly pristine nestled in their clear plastic case. Once she opened them, they'd never be perfect again.

Mary-Kate, you have trouble with beginnings and endings, her granny always said kindly, *but you're very good with in-betweens.* Mary-Kate took a deep breath and closed her eyes again. Maybe she could just keep them closed for the rest of the day.

'Mary-Kate,' said Professor Martin, who'd looked up from the *Archaeology Monthly* magazine she was reading. 'I know you can do this.'

Mary-Kate opened her eyes.

Did her mother mean go on an unexpected archaeology trip, or open the pens? Or something else? Professor Martin had the determined gleam in her eyes that she often wore. She was a strong woman, always disappearing on adventures to strange locations: jungles and deserts and remote mountain ranges. Mary-Kate wished she was like her mother.

The Professor must mean the pens.

'Yes, I know I can,' Mary-Kate said and tried to add that same determined glint to her eyes as she opened the pens with a small click. The train did not suddenly crash. London, grey and miserable, kept sliding past the windows in a blur.

The geography project was to draw and name the peaks of the Swiss Alps. The Swiss Alps were very jagged in the image Mary-Kate had copied from her mobile phone, so she attempted to make them look a little neater, rounding off the pointiest parts. She coloured them in purple and yellow because those were complementary colours. Outside, the grey city gave way to green fields. The train rushed through the countryside, little towns passing fleetingly.

'So, this town is called Woolington Well?' she asked tentatively, once she was satisfied that the alps looked much better. The train still hadn't crashed since she'd opened the glitter pens, so that was a positive. It had kept speeding on through the countryside.

'Yes, it is,' said Professor Martin. 'And a large shopping centre is to be built there. A small action group have applied for a stop work order because they believe a place of historical significance has been partially destroyed. An old well. They believe that there are bones present.'

'What kind of bones?'

'I can't be sure until I've looked at them. They also reported pottery in the same location, so maybe it was once a burial ground. Or maybe it could be something more mysterious,' she said. 'You know how I like mysterious. Now wouldn't that be exciting on your first trip!'

Mary-Kate smiled but she secretly hoped it was a very un-mysterious type of trip. She didn't think she'd be very good at mysterious. She was better at facts. Facts made her feel almost as comfortable as the shopping channel and thirty-minute infomercials on vegetable slicers. Still, something about those words *bones* and *burial ground* had given her butterflies.

Maybe going on a work trip with her mother *would* be interesting.

'Will I get to watch you?' she asked.

'Well, you can,' said Professor Martin, 'or you might like to go exploring too. I think the country air will do you the world of good.'

Mary-Kate tried to picture herself exploring but had to stop. A lot of things went wrong for explorers. They became lost. They ran out of water. They were chased by tigers. They went up mountains and never came back.

She took a deep breath, unzipped her backpack and retrieved her lucky globe stress ball. *Everything will be fine, Mary-Kate*, she said silently to herself. She picked up a glitter pen and added a raspberry glitter outline to each alp.

'Oh, and I forgot to say,' said Professor Martin, lifting her magazine again and sliding her glasses back up her nose, 'the man who is building the shopping centre, Lord Woolington, has invited us for lunch. At his country house. Apparently, it has its own maze!'

The train rushed through the countryside. The sky was a brilliant blue and Mary-Kate leaned her cheek against the window to look up at the sun. She would not think of exploring. Or being lost on mountain sides. Or her father. She would not think of Bartley Towers or the jaggedness of the Swiss Alps. She would not think of beginnings and glitter pens that had lost their perfectness.

She breathed in and out the way she'd been taught.

She listened for five things that she could hear, an exercise her counsellor, Meg, had taught her. The sound of the train. A man opposite them opening a can. A page turning. The compartment door opening. A cough.

Five things she could feel. Her feet in her favourite red sparkly shoes. Her black woollen stockings on her legs. The window glass against her cheek. The raspberry glitter pen in her hand. The little lucky ring her granny had given her, which she wore on her finger.

Five things she could see. The sun. A distant church spire. A flock of sheep. A stone wall. One lone dark cloud far on the horizon. She noticed her own reflection, right there in the window, staring back at her. Her favourite black hair bow, her long brown hair.

There, that felt better.

'I'm going to try to look forward to visiting Woolington Well,' she said softly, and Professor Martin smiled at her.

There are, though, several small items that a monster hunter finds indispensable. The first of these will be useful in numerous situations: an umbrella.

P.K. Mayberry's Complete Guide to Monsters of the Northern Hemisphere

Professor Martin held her large black umbrella over them as they trudged with their suitcases along the muddy lane. They had arrived at an empty train station, the representative from the shopping centre absent, and when they both checked their phones, they discovered there was no mobile service. A flock of damp sheep watched them in a bored fashion.

'Well, I said it would be exciting, didn't I?' laughed Professor Martin, as they set off towards a distant collection of buildings nestled in the fields.

Apart from the misty rain, which showed no sign of abating, the countryside was very pretty, and Mary-Kate was glad for it. It really didn't look like the sort of place where anything could ever go wrong. It was postcard perfect. They crossed a little arched bridge that spanned a small burbling stream and passed the village green, surrounded by peaceful spreading oaks. A little church spire peeked through the thatched rooftops and the cottages had yards filled with tumbling roses and hollyhocks.

Behind the village a large round hill rose, covered in boulders, but Mary-Kate decided it didn't look like the sort of hill there could be an avalanche on. Nearby it, there stood a large old stately home. Even from a distance Mary-Kate could tell it was very grand. It had many windows and great stone pillars at its entrance and a driveway flanked by manicured gardens.

'I guess that's Woolington House,' said Mary-Kate, pointing.

'I think you guess right.' Professor Martin checked her phone. 'Still no service. The hotel is called the Hook and Worm. The village is tiny so I'm sure it won't be too hard to find.'

Mary-Kate looked up and down the entrance to each lane that they passed. There were several tiny teashops, all of them closed. A bakery with a sign on its door that read, ONLY OPEN ON SATURDAYS. An art gallery that was closed too. It was charming and perfect, but as they walked, Mary-Kate was beginning to notice something else.

Woolington Well was very quiet.

The birds were singing and the river chattering beneath the bridge they'd crossed, and faraway there was the sound of traffic on the M1, but Woolington Well itself seemed very still. Not a single person to be seen. Nothing open. Mary-Kate's red sparkly shoes clicked loudly on the wet cobblestones.

And even stranger, Mary-Kate noticed by the front door of every dear little cottage there sat a saucer of milk.

'Prof, why's there a saucer of milk on every doorstep?' asked Mary-Kate. Her voice sounded loud in the stillness.

'Well-spotted, Mary-Kate,' said Professor Martin. 'Why do you think there might be?'

Mary-Kate's mother liked her to think critically.

'Cats drink milk from saucers, I guess,' said Mary-Kate. 'There must be an awful lot of cats in Woolington Well. Oh, look, here! It's the Hook & Wyrm Inn, only they've spelled worm strangely.'

They stood before an old country inn, its name on a small sign near its heavy wooden front door: **THE HOOK & WYRM INN.** And there wasn't just a saucer of milk near the front door of this establishment. There was a large pail of milk instead.

'That's very strange,' said Mary-Kate.

'Maybe the mystery of the milk is something you can solve while in Woolington, Mary-Kate.'

The mystery of the milk.

That doesn't seem too daunting, thought Mary-Kate.

She could probably do small mysteries.

'Challenge accepted,' she said as Professor Martin pushed opened the front door.

Mary-Kate was thinking about saucers of milk and why someone had spelled 'Wyrm' with a 'Y'. She was glad she'd packed her strawberry-scented notebook because a notebook would probably be helpful when solving problems. She'd continue using the glitter pens now that she'd succeeded in opening them.

It was a cosy pub filled with the aroma of polished wood and a warm fire burning in the corner of the small dining room. It was also empty. Or at least it appeared to be. Professor Martin coughed politely and when no one appeared, she rang the bell at the counter. It echoed in the silence.

To their surprise, a bald head appeared from behind the counter. The man stood up, looking very nervous, eyes darting to the door and windows and back again. His name tag said 'TERRY' and despite his bald head he had a bushy red beard.

'My apologies,' he said. 'I thought it was …'

He stopped, wrung his hands anxiously, laughed a nervous laugh.

'You must be Professor Martin,' he said. 'Welcome to Woolington Well. We are so glad you are here.'

'Thank you,' said Professor Martin. 'We're very pleased to be here.'

'You have the Woolington suite for two nights,' he said, handing over a key. Mary-Kate noticed his hands were trembling. 'I hope it will be comfortable for you.'

'I'm sure it will be most comfortable,' said the Professor.

'And Ms Honey, the village librarian, says she will be here at eleven,' he added, looking like at any moment he was going to disappear behind the counter.

'Oh, I didn't know I was meeting the village librarian,' said the Professor, glancing at the clock on the wall behind the counter. It was almost eleven.

'She hopes to catch you before Lord Woolington arrives. I'm sure she wants to talk to you about the ...' He twitched violently as a cloud cast a sudden shadow over the doorway behind them. 'About the you-know-what.'

'Of course,' said Professor Martin, very kindly.

As they climbed the narrow creaking steps to their room, Mary-Kate whispered to her mother:

'Do you know what he was talking about?'

'Not exactly,' said Professor Martin. 'Although I feel we are about to find out.'

The Woolington suite at the Hook & Wyrm Inn was the most luxurious room that Mary-Kate had ever seen. There were two large four-poster beds draped in gold velvet curtains, sumptuous deep red carpets and two chairs before a roaring fireplace. A huge tapestry hung on the wall.

'Well this is something, isn't it?' said Professor Martin.

'Do you always stay in places like this?' said Mary-Kate.

'Unfortunately not,' laughed her mother.

Mary-Kate moved slowly in awe around the large suite. There was a tea stand in one corner, filled with small cakes and sandwiches and, nearby, a teapot in a cosy. There was a bookshelf that reached to the ceiling, containing hundreds of old books, encyclopedias and histories and famous novels. She ran her finger along the spines. She'd never been in a hotel room that had its own library. The bathroom contained a deep bath with golden claw feet. She touched the little toiletries in pretty glass bottles. She unwrapped the chocolate on her pillow, popped it into her mouth and flopped onto the bed. She would be happy to stay and be an explorer, right here in this room.

From the window beside her bed there was a view of the strange round hill and the grand country house, and she noticed that this view was repeated in the tapestry that hung on the opposite wall. It was richly woven in blues, greens and golds, and showed a scene of the village. There was the church spire she'd seen, and the little arched bridge over the winding stream, the round hill and the country house. She had just spotted a small figure in the foreground standing on the little arched bridge with a fishing line when there was a frantic rapping at the door.

A small dark-haired woman leaped into the room when the door was opened by Professor Martin.

'Wonderful,' the woman said, taking a deep shuddering breath as though she'd run a race. 'Great. I'm here in time. Do you mind if I—?'

She lurched forwards and closed the curtains.

Ms Honey was tiny, not much taller than Mary-Kate. She didn't look old enough to be a librarian. Her spiky black hair was in disarray and her bright pink glasses were lopsided. She wore black jeans and sneakers and a T-shirt emblazoned with the words 'NO TO THE WOOLINGTON SHOPPING CENTRE'. She was trembling all over and trying to calm down her breathing.

'I'm Yolanda Honey. Village librarian. Secretary of the Say No to the Shopping Centre Action Group and president of the Wyrm Watch Society.'

Despite all these titles, Mary-Kate thought Yolanda Honey still looked like she wanted to dive under the bed.

'Please sit down Ms Honey,' said Professor Martin, who was always very polite. 'Can we get you a cup of tea?'

Ms Honey didn't sit down. She lifted the edge of a curtain and peeked out the window.

'Please call me Yolanda. You should keep these shut,' she added, 'and it's probably best you keep the little one inside. What's your name?'

'Mary-Kate,' said Mary-Kate. She wasn't sure she liked being called a little one, considering she was almost ten. And what on earth was Ms Honey talking about? Mary-Kate smiled politely like her mother though.

'Are you feeling all right, Yolanda?' asked Professor Martin with concern. 'Would you like sugar in your tea?'

'It's children,' said Yolanda. 'The legend says it likes children you see, Professor Martin.'

'No, I don't see,' said Professor Martin calmly. 'Please explain what you mean.'

'I'll show you.' Yolanda was reaching in her

handbag to retrieve a folded newspaper when there was another loud knock at the door.

Mary-Kate opened it this time and found a tall man in a grey suit leaning against the wall. He wore a flower in his lapel and his fair hair flopped over his blue eyes. He was grinning broadly.

'Hello Miss Martin,' he said, shaking Mary-Kate's hand briskly and moving into the room. 'My sincerest apologies. There was a mix-up with your collection from the train station. Lord Woolington. Hello, Professor, so glad you could come, and in such a timely manner. The foundation concrete is to be poured tomorrow so we need this all sorted out as quickly as possible. Oh, and the delightful Ms Honey too! What a lovely surprise.'

He was loud and friendly and had shaken everyone's hands before they had time to reply. Mary-Kate noticed that Yolanda didn't seem to like having her hand shaken. She had shrunk back against the curtains with a frown. Lord Woolington flashed her a charming smile.

'I have the car waiting downstairs,' he said. 'Shall we? Ms Honey, of course you are most welcome to join us for lunch too.'

'Ms Honey was about to show us something,' said Professor Martin. 'If you could give us a moment?'

'Oh, no, no,' said Yolanda, pushing her way past Lord Woolington as though she couldn't bear to be in the same room as him. 'I'll be sure to return. Here's my card.'

She handed it to Mary-Kate, who was closest. Mary-Kate noticed a pleading expression in her eyes as she rushed from the room. *The legend says it likes children*, Mary-Kate repeated silently to herself as she picked up her sparkly red backpack and placed the card in the front pocket. She extracted her lucky globe stress ball and squeezed it several times. Professor Martin placed a comforting hand on her shoulder as they followed Lord Woolington down the stairs.

Lord Woolington motioned to several landmarks in the village as he ferried them in his expensive Bentley. The rain had stopped, and the sun was shining. He pointed down a laneway to where Mary-Kate caught a glimpse of heavy machinery and scaffolding.

'Down there will be the beating heart of Woolington Well and the entire county,' he said. 'And I'll be very pleased to have this whole mess with the bones cleared up by you, Professor Martin.'

He gestured at the small closed teashops as he steered the car out of the village. It turned out, he owned them all.

'There will be a food court in the shopping centre,' he said. 'People will want to move here to be near the centre, of course, so these will revert to cottages.'

He pointed out a small hotel, which was also his. Then a retirement home proudly owned by the Woolington family. Woolington Green, where the Woolington Cricket Club, proudly sponsored by the Woolington family, played on weekends.

'We have big plans for that space with all the

developments,' said Lord Woolington cheerily, pointing to the peaceful village green surrounded by large oaks that Mary-Kate had glimpsed on her walk into the village.

He smiled at Mary-Kate in the rear-view mirror. Lord Woolington was very friendly, but there was something about him that made Mary-Kate uneasy. She wasn't sure what it was, so she squeezed the stress ball. Perhaps it was his loudness. Loud voices sometimes made her feel worried. Amelia Blythe-Tompkinson at school was very loud and as soon as Mary-Kate heard her voice, she froze and forgot how to talk properly.

Lord Woolington turned the car over the small bridge and out into the fields.

'That, of course, is Round Hill,' he said, pointing to the small round hill across the fields. 'All part of the village legends that you'll hear about soon enough.'

He laughed loudly at this and Mary-Kate wondered why.

She extracted her strawberry-scented notebook

from her sparkly backpack as they drove out through the green fields. She opened the pen case as well and took out a lemon-coloured glitter pen. She felt she needed to write something down. It seemed very important. There was something going on here, something bigger than the mystery of the saucers of milk that the Prof had asked her to solve.

Still, at the top of the first page of the notebook, she wrote:

Saucers of Milk?

Followed by:

'The legend says it likes children.'

In neat quotation marks.

She then added:

Yolanda Honey, President of Worm Watch Society.

Also:

Why is 'Wyrm' at the Hook & Wyrm Inn spelled with a 'Y'?

This had been bothering her ever since she saw the Hook & Wyrm's sign.

And finally:

Round Hill, part of the village legends?

It seemed like a very odd collection of statements and questions, but something about writing them down made her feel calmer. She placed her globe stress ball back into her backpack.

Lord Woolington was crossing another small bridge then and speeding along the grand entrance drive to Woolington House. The road was flanked by grand old trees and the house loomed ahead of them, grey and imposing.

'Woolington House,' he declared as they pulled to a stop. 'The original house burned down in the sixteenth century but this one has been here since 1720.'

'Impressive Georgian example,' remarked Professor Martin as they climbed out of the car and stood before the house.

Mary-Kate looked up at the many windows, all gleaming in the new sunshine. There must have been

at least fifty, she was sure. So many windows and so many rooms, yet if houses could have emotions, she'd say Woolington House was definitely lonely. It stood staring straight ahead, so blankly that it made her shiver.

'Please, follow me,' said Lord Woolington, taking the steps two at a time up towards the entrance.

Mary-Kate hesitated. Some movement in one of the windows had caught her eye. On the third floor in the corner of one of the great sash windows there was a little face peering down at her. A girl's face.

'Mary-Kate,' called Professor Martin from the doorway.

'Coming!'

When Mary-Kate looked back to the window the face was gone.

Lunch was served in a glass conservatory at the rear of the house. They walked for a very long time to get there, across marble floors, through large richly decorated rooms, past gilt-edged frames containing paintings of Woolingtons past. Mary-Kate had a sneaking suspicion there might have been a quicker way. Lord Woolington seemed to enjoy showing them through his very large house. He pointed out numerous artefacts as they went. A precious clock. An urn that was four hundred years old. A painting of his great-great-great-great-great-grandfather, who had built the house. He looked very similar to the present-day Lord. Through the large glass conservatory windows, there was a view of a hedge maze and rising rather dramatically behind it, because they were much closer to it now, Round Hill was perfectly framed.

'I like most of what great-great-great-great-great-grandpapa did, but having Round Hill as the view from the conservatory was probably not his best design idea,' said Lord Woolington. 'I'm wondering if it could be bulldozed while we have the heavy earth-moving equipment in the village.'

Professor Martin looked shocked by this and Lord Woolington guffawed again.

'I'm joking, of course,' he declared. 'Please sit down.'

Two staff members entered the room carrying silver trays. One held an impressive array of sandwiches, the other a tea service. Mary-Kate hoped they weren't complicated sandwiches and that she wouldn't have to make small talk. Complicated sandwiches and small talk were two of her least favourite things.

'Thank you,' she said, taking a simple cheese and pickle sandwich and breathing a sigh of relief.

'The Woolington Shopping Centre has been years in the planning,' began Lord Woolington, once the tea was poured. 'I'm so glad you came today so that I could tell you about it. As you know, it is to be situated at the heart of Woolington Well in the old town square and folk will come from across parishes to shop here!'

Mary-Kate chewed thoughtfully and watched Lord Woolington. If he was normally loud, he was now definitely shouting as he started to talk about the shopping centre. His eyes gleamed with pride.

'It will be a sight to behold. Two magnificent levels – groceries downstairs, clothes and a toy department up top – lots of glass, a state-of-the-art escalator,' he continued. 'I can show you the plans.'

Mary-Kate tried to imagine a huge glass building at the heart of that quaint little village. It didn't seem possible. She was jolted back by Lord Woolington's voice, which had grown even louder.

'And, of course, on these plans I can point out where these rather inconvenient items that have been located during excavation are situated so that we can clean this business up as quickly as possible. As I mentioned, the concrete trucks will be arriving in the morning. The deadline for pouring is five tomorrow afternoon.'

'It will be most helpful to see the plans,' said Professor Martin pleasantly, although Mary-Kate could tell from the slight change in her voice that she was not happy. One thing her mother didn't like was being rushed or influenced in any way. Whether it was choosing an item in a shop or the way to approach an archaeological excavation or deciding whether Mary-Kate could watch fifteen minutes of the shopping channel.

Sensing this change, Lord Woolington folded

his napkin and smiled his charming smile.

'Glorious weather,' he said. 'I'm so glad the sun has come out for your visit.'

Mary-Kate's heart sank.

Here came the small talk.

She tried to slide down her chair slightly so she wouldn't be included.

Small talk made her stomach twist because she wasn't any good at it. No matter how much she watched other people do it she could never master it. She could never think of the right thing to say and not knowing the right thing to say made her feel like she was failing an exam. She'd decided it was almost entirely the reason she was having such a terrible time at Bartley Towers. When Amelia Blythe-Tompkinson and her friends made loud small talk about dancing and pop stars, Mary-Kate never knew the correct thing to say.

'Do you like shopping, Mary-Kate?' asked Lord Woolington. 'Perhaps we can have you back to the grand opening.'

'I like online shopping,' said Mary-Kate, 'and on the shopping channel.'

Lord Woolington looked very disappointed. Mary-Kate's stomach sank. Of course, she should have said she loved shopping, especially shopping in large double-storey village shopping centres. She wished she had her stress ball. What was she thinking putting it away in her backpack?

'Perhaps you could show me these plans?' said Professor Martin, changing the subject.

Lord Woolington stood up and retrieved papers from a side table. He cleared a space on the table and laid them out, grinning as he did so. He seemed to love everything and anything to do with this shopping centre, even if it was only drawings of it.

'See here? The old market square is where the foundations of the centre are being laid. The village green – you'll remember I mentioned it – well we're currently designing a multi-storey car park to be constructed on it. There will be a suspended walkway built from the car park to the supermarket.'

Lord Woolington looked very happy about this fact.

'A car park?' repeated Mary-Kate. She hadn't meant to say it aloud.

'Yes, there will be many visitors and the lanes are narrow. This is the perfect space!' said Lord Woolington, raking his hair back from his eyes, obviously delighted.

Mary-Kate thought of the glimpse she'd had of the green, as they'd walked into the village. She thought of the oak trees. She thought of the birds that lived in them.

'Pardon?' she managed.

Surely the trees won't be bulldozed, she thought. Perhaps the trees would be removed and planted somewhere else? *La-la-la-la-la-la-la*, she said silently to herself to stop thinking these thoughts. She felt Professor Martin put a hand on her shoulder. Lord Woolington was talking about a well now. A well in the market square. A well that was the source of all his problems.

'Mary-Kate, perhaps you could go and look at

the maze?' suggested Professor Martin. 'Would that be all right, Lord Woolington?'

'Of course!' he cried. 'Please, through that door over there.'

'Get some fresh air,' said her mother as she handed Mary-Kate her backpack and guided her away from the map. 'Don't think about it.'

'What about the—' began Mary-Kate, as her mother opened the door and put a finger to her lips.

'Later,' Professor Martin interrupted.

Outside, the sun was shining brightly and Mary-Kate was glad for it. She closed her eyes and willed the thought of those trees away. *I can't think of you*, she said to herself. *I have to do my breathing.* With her eyes closed, she reached into her backpack and extracted her stress ball.

'Why do you have your eyes closed?' asked a voice.

'Oh!' cried Mary-Kate, opening them to find a girl standing before her. It was the same girl she'd seen in the window. She had a small face, smudged with dirt, surrounded by a halo of frizzy blonde hair.

'I needed to rest my eyes. It's very sunny out here.'

'I'm Lady Arabella Woolington,' said the girl. She was dressed in mud-stained moleskins and a riding jacket. 'I was riding Pickles.'

'Pickles?' said Mary-Kate, surprised.

'My pony.' Arabella Woolington smiled brightly. 'Would you like to meet him?'

A monster hunter should always
remember that their allies will come
in many shapes and forms.

*P.K. Mayberry's Complete Guide to
Monsters of the Northern Hemisphere*

Pickles was a stout pony with a round belly who did not look impressed that he had a saddle on his back. His tail swished from side to side as he chewed grass.

'We came last in dressage and second-last in showjumping on Saturday,' said Arabella proudly. 'Pickles doesn't really like jumping.'

Pickles looked like he only liked eating, and even then, he seemed quite cross about it.

'Have you got a pony?' asked Arabella.

Mary-Kate shook her head. She'd only attended pony club for a term at Bartley Towers.

'If you had one, what would you call it?' continued Arabella. She was very talkative. Mary-Kate tried desperately to think of a good horse name. She didn't want to say the wrong thing.

'How about Mayonnaise?' said Arabella, deciding for her with a giggle. 'If he was white, of course.'

'Maybe,' said Mary-Kate.

'I'm not allowed a new pony that's better at jumping,' said Arabella sadly. 'Is your mother a very important archaeologist? Has she been to Egypt and found a mummy?'

This was the question Mary-Kate was most asked when people discovered her mother was an archaeologist.

'Not really. I mean, she's been to Egypt, although mostly she found cooking utensils.'

Arabella looked every bit as disappointed as Lord Woolington when Mary-Kate had mentioned online shopping. 'Oh well, maybe she will one day,' said Arabella, hopefully. 'Papa says she definitely won't find anything exciting in Woolington Well, but …'

Arabella stopped and patted Pickles's nose as though she was thinking.

'But what?' prompted Mary-Kate.

'Nothing,' said Arabella and then she giggled again. 'I was only thinking, wouldn't it be exciting if she *did* find something interesting? Then it would be on the nightly news and I could ride by on Pickles and wave at the camera.'

Mary-Kate giggled too, though something in Arabella's bright blue eyes told Mary-Kate that this wasn't really what she had been about to say.

'Would you like to pat him?' Arabella quickly changed the subject. 'Or would you like to go in the maze? I know, I could show you my doll's house!'

'I guess,' said Mary-Kate, hoping with all her might that she wasn't going to be made to play with it. She followed Arabella back into the house and up a grand staircase, Arabella chattering the whole way about the doll's house and how it once belonged to her great-grandmother, and how it had real working electric lights and was an exact replica of Woolington House.

The doll's house was almost as big as Mary-Kate's bedroom.

'I wasn't expecting that,' said Mary-Kate.

Arabella looked very pleased.

It stood as tall as them and the windows burned bright with electric lights. A toy Bentley was parked in the drive and there was a painted river that ran across the front grounds, like the one they'd crossed with the small arched bridge.

'Look, that doll even has a little fishing rod,' said Mary-Kate, in awe.

'That's James Woolington.' Arabella smiled and leaned in close to whisper, 'He's fishing for the wyrm. Don't tell papa.'

'The worm?' Mary-Kate looked at the little doll with the fishing line stuck down to the painted blue water with glue. *The Hook and Wyrm. Worm*

Watch Society. She wished she could take out her strawberry-scented notebook and show Arabella the questions she'd written down. Maybe Arabella could answer some of them.

Or maybe she'd laugh.

'We mustn't mention the wyrm,' said Arabella, almost to herself, before turning on another dazzling smile. 'Help me open it up? I'll show you how the toilets flush.'

'Please let her stay,' Lady Arabella Woolington had cried when the maid arrived to inform them that Professor Martin and Mary-Kate were being returned to the Hook & Wyrm by a driver. Mary-Kate had only just witnessed the amazing feat of flushing doll's house toilets.

'Can't she stay?' she'd begged her father at the front door. He patted her on the head and laughed.

'We'll have Mary-Kate back for tea again, shall we?' he said. Mary-Kate noticed the offer was not extended to her mother. Professor Martin nodded curtly to Lord Woolington as she got into the car.

The driver was a dignified-looking man with silvery hair. He introduced himself as Graham.

'What do you think of Woolington Well?' he asked.

'Very pretty indeed,' said Professor Martin politely.

For the time being, thought Mary-Kate, imagining the shopping centre and the floating walkway and the car park instead of the beautiful old oaks. They made the short trip back to Woolington Well in silence, crossing the little bridge that Mary-Kate had seen before in the doll's house.

She opened her backpack and took out her strawberry-scented notebook. She added **James Woolington** to her list, followed by several lime-green glitter pen question marks.

She had so many questions for her mother, who seemed deep in thought, staring out the window. Mary-Kate touched her mother's sleeve and showed her the page. The Prof nodded approvingly.

Mary-Kate noticed that Graham was watching them in the rear-view mirror, so she hurriedly put the notebook away.

Inside the Hook & Wyrm Inn, the concierge Terry stood up from his hiding place behind the counter and smiled apologetically.

'Hello Terry,' said Professor Martin. 'Any messages?'

'Yes, this was left for you by Ms Honey,' he replied, hurriedly handing her a note.

'Thank you,' said Professor Martin. 'I will be in the village square working this afternoon. Can you recommend any nearby landmarks that Mary-Kate could visit?'

Terry looked shocked by this question. Mary-Kate noticed beads of sweat emerge on his forehead.

'Well, I'm not sure,' he stammered. 'Maybe it's best if she … there are some board games in the corner of the dining room near the fireplace.'

'That's very helpful,' nodded Professor Martin.

Upstairs, Mary-Kate flung herself onto her four-poster bed. What on earth was going on in this village? Why was there a pail of milk left at the front door of the Hook & Wyrm Inn? Why was 'Wyrm' spelled with a 'Y'? Why had Arabella said *we mustn't mention the worm*? What was Terry so scared of? This was the strangest place she'd ever visited. Her mother, who had her suitcase open and was extracting her work implements, paused and smiled at Mary-Kate.

'I liked the questions in your notebook, Mary-Kate,' she said. 'I'm wondering if there is some helpful information in that newspaper that Ms Honey left behind on the chair.'

Mary-Kate jumped up.

Yolanda Honey had left behind the newspaper she'd been going to show them when Lord Woolington arrived. It was folded neatly on the armrest. Under the Sport banner there was a headline about the Woolington Cricket Club's battle to survive once their green became a car park. Lord Woolington had offered to make a new green in the grounds of Woolington House. Mary-Kate knew sport was always in the last pages of a newspaper. She flipped the paper over to the front page and unfolded it.

WOOLINGTON WARBLER
IS THE WYRM BACK?

Could the Woolington Wyrm have reappeared after nearly a century? Sunday night, frightened Woolington Well residents heard loud noises and found a fence flattened and coated in slime.

There have been accounts of Woolington Wyrm sightings since the thirteenth century. There are also numerous versions of the legend. Most start with a young man by the name of James Woolington who went fishing and caught a strange creature in the river Ormer.

This creature was said to be eel-like, and even stranger: it could breathe out of water. James Woolington hid this creature in the village well with plans to show his brothers when they came home from battle in France. Unfortunately, his brothers did not return from war, and the creature was forgotten.

Many years later, a huge serpent-like monster began to terrorise the countryside around the village of Woolington Well. Some said it breathed fire. Others said its breath was poisonous or that it liked to hunt cows and sheep at night. This creature was named the Woolington Wyrm.

Over centuries, there have been many stories told of the villagers' attempts to rid the countryside of the wyrm. Varying accounts have it living in the village well, recently damaged by construction work, or the nearby landmark, Round Hill. Sunday night was the first time there have been signs of the creature in nearly a century.

One eyewitness, who refused to be named, said he heard a large screech before dawn. When he raced outside, he saw a ball of flame shooting into the sky.

Lord Woolington went on record to state, 'It's all nonsense. Everyone knows such things aren't real. This village is building the largest shopping centre in the county, which will draw hundreds of visitors to the area. And here we are talking about nonsense. Woolington needs to wake up to itself.'

Mary-Kate stood for several seconds digesting this information, words buzzing in her head. A wyrm.

A Woolington. A well. A war. She closed her eyes. The wyrm was some sort of large creature. A large serpent-like creature. A large cow-eating creature that breathed fire.

She *really* had not been expecting that.

She had been expecting something small and wriggly.

This was a big change. She checked herself to see if she felt anxious. Her breathing was normal. She sifted through the story in her head and located the word 'slime'. *A fence flattened and coated in slime.*

Mary-Kate didn't like slime. Not any slime. Even if slime was colour coordinated and sparkly, she would not like it. She didn't even like the word 'slime', which sounded like what slime looked like in her mind. A flattened fence coated in slime should make her very anxious.

She took a deep breath. Perhaps if she didn't think about the fence and the slime it would be better. She opened her eyes to see her mother watching her.

'Everything all right, Mary-Kate?'

'I think so,' said Mary-Kate. 'I wasn't expecting a legend about a large serpent. Or …'

She couldn't bring herself to say the word 'slime'.

'Any answers to your questions? Or maybe only more questions?' asked Professor Martin.

'I think more questions,' said Mary-Kate. Surprisingly, this made her feel a small tremor of excitement.

'No such thing as a bad question,' said Professor Martin, who liked Mary-Kate to use critical thinking to help her overcome some of her anxieties. 'In fact, I'm off to ask some myself. There are no answers unless you ask questions, right?'

She had her work equipment and her brown broad-brimmed hat on.

'Can I come?' asked Mary-Kate.

'Why don't you go exploring and keep solving the mystery of the milk? Although I expect it's a much bigger mystery than that now, isn't it?' Professor Martin took Mary-Kate's face in her hands and kissed her on the forehead. 'Good luck.'

She was almost at the door before she turned quickly. 'I nearly forgot! You might be interested in this, I think.'

She handed Mary-Kate the note that had been left at the front desk by Ms Honey and then clicked the hotel door shut behind her. Mary-Kate unfolded the small rectangle of paper.

Emergency Meeting of the Wyrm Watch Society, 2 pm. Village Library. All Welcome.

Mary-Kate sat on the four-poster bed with the note in her hand. James Woolington was the man in the legend. She could answer that question at least. And 'Wyrm' was spelled with a 'Y' because, well, it wasn't a worm at all. It was something much larger from a legend. And some people were saying that the wyrm was nonsense while others were saying that the wyrm had returned and now the Wyrm Watch Society were having an emergency meeting. It was probably the best place to go to find information about the wyrm.

If she needed information about the wyrm.

She looked at the words in her notebook. **'The legend says it likes children.'**

That worried her.

Maybe it was better if she didn't think about the wyrm at all? Really, she'd only said she was going to solve the small mystery of the milk. She could just as easily go downstairs and ask Terry about that and then sit in the nice hotel suite and eat cakes and look at the books on the bookshelf.

She looked at the tapestry on the wall beside her bed. She looked at the pretty little village of Woolington and grey, lonely Woolington House and that little figure in the foreground, fishing from the bridge.

That's James Woolington fishing for the wyrm. Don't tell Papa.

'Oh!' she said. It was a small, exasperated *oh*.

She didn't know if she was any good at solving large mysteries. She mightn't know how. She might be bad at it, like knowing pop songs or dance moves. She squeezed her lucky stress ball. It didn't seem to help. This required something luckier than the stress ball.

This was a big change. This was a beginning.

Mary-Kate, you have trouble with beginnings and endings, but you're very good with in-betweens.

All she need do was *begin*. And the best way to begin was to attend the Emergency Meeting of the Wyrm Watch Society, which was in fifteen minutes' time. She opened her suitcase and found the lucky silver packet containing the last seven pieces of gum her father left behind before he disappeared. She held the packet in her hands and closed her eyes.

What would he do?

Mary-Kate had been told he was also an archaeologist. A mountaineer and an explorer too.

That he had parachuted into jungles and trekked to the North Pole. He spoke several languages and could decipher hieroglyphics in the blink of an eye. He did big things. Huge things. Brave things.

These were the things that she'd been told. What she remembered was his smile. The way he chewed his gum and smiled at her.

The lavender smell of his dark hair.

The way he balanced her on his shoulders so she could see the whole world.

What would he do?

She opened her eyes and placed the silver packet in her black dress pocket and patted it three times. She opened her red sparkly backpack and added her lucky international coin collection, her lucky novelty Big Ben torch and her first- and second-favourite lucky oversized handkerchiefs.

He'd go to the Emergency Meeting of the Wyrm Watch Society, of course.

So that's what Mary-Kate would do.

A monster hunter's
greatest tool is knowledge.

*P.K. Mayberry's Complete Guide to
Monsters of the Northern Hemisphere*

Mary-Kate's red shoes sparkled in the sunlight as she walked through the empty village. She had decided that it was best not to think too much about this big beginning, so she concentrated on her shoes instead. Of all the colours that a sparkle could be added to, red was her favourite. Red sparkles made her feel calm, the same way that unused soap bars did, or neatly stacked silver spoons, or thirty-minute infomercials on vacuums.

So far, the beginning had not gone well. She'd needed a map of the village to find the library, but when she opened her phone there was still no service. Also, Terry, who she thought might have a map, seemed to have completely disappeared from downstairs. *It's only a small village*, she had told herself, in a soothing voice. *It won't be too hard to find.* She wandered in the direction of the construction she'd glimpsed from Lord Woolington's car. Libraries were often in the middle of places, she'd decided. Like town halls and squares.

There were lots of large signs the closer she came to the village centre and the construction site. She saw a small forest of scaffolding arising behind tall chain-wire fencing. It was a depressing scene.

The small cottages at the edge of the village square had their windows boarded over and the flowers in their gardens were untended, wilted. A sign for a teashop had collapsed onto the cobblestones and

no one had bothered to pick it up. Someone had left behind their lunch wrappers and they blew in small circles across the lane. But she noticed something else too. At the door of every rundown derelict cottage, there was a saucer of milk.

She peered through the fence surrounding the construction site. Everywhere there was the rubble

of rock and torn-up cobblestones. Huge trenches had been dug by diggers, which sat idle. And there, in the middle of what remained of the square, was her mother standing waist-deep in a hole. Three construction workers stood nearby, watching. Even from a distance, Mary-Kate could tell these people were worried, peering anxiously into the hole. As though sensing Mary-Kate was somewhere nearby, Professor Martin looked up and waved. She did not seem worried at all.

'Do you know where the library is?' called Mary-Kate.

She watched her mother consult with one of the workers, a woman in a hard hat, who pointed across the ruins of the market square.

'There's a sign at the entrance to each lane that runs off the square,' called back Professor Martin. 'You'll come to it if you walk that way.'

'Thank you,' said Mary-Kate, waving, trying to look brave.

She squeezed herself through a small space left

between the construction and cottage garden fences, in the direction her mother had pointed. There were several exits into small winding lanes and each of them contained signs pointing to village landmarks. One said TO ROUND HILL. Another said VILLAGE GREEN. *Not for much longer*, thought Mary-Kate, remembering the car park plans and the oak trees.

A large sign read: TO HISTORIC WOOLINGTON HOUSE

'Been there, done that,' said Mary-Kate quietly.

Finally, at the next laneway entrance there was a sign pointing to the village library. It was a small stone building, so old that it leaned. The curtains in its windows were drawn. A noticeboard near the front door was plastered with details of the Say No to the Shopping Centre Action Group. Mary-Kate felt a flutter of nerves. It was nearly two o'clock. The meeting would begin soon. She'd never been to a proper meeting. They were probably a bit like group projects at Bartley Towers, which were terrifying.

Also, she'd probably have to make small talk. She hoped there was a big crowd and she could creep in quietly and sit unnoticed at the back.

She pushed open the front door and it made such a loud creak that the four people seated in a circle at the centre of the library looked up in unison. There was definitely not a large crowd at the Emergency Meeting of the Wyrm Watch Society.

'Mary-Kate,' whispered Yolanda Honey, leaping up.

'Everyone, this is the daughter of Professor Martin, who arrived today to examine the well because of the stop work order we submitted,' she continued in a hushed voice. Then, to Mary-Kate: 'Please join us.'

Yolanda grabbed a chair and placed it in the small circle. The library was shadowy with the curtains drawn, but Mary-Kate immediately recognised two of those seated: Terry the concierge and Graham, Lord Woolington's driver. No wonder Terry had been missing from the front desk. He still looked very scared.

Mary-Kate waved shyly, then wished she hadn't,

because maybe no one waved at meetings. She sat down quickly in the chair offered to her.

'I'm Moira Lewis,' whispered the woman beside her. She had a large array of corkscrew curls sprouting from the bandana on her head. 'The baker. Or was, until half the village was dug up.'

'That's the problem, isn't it?' said Graham. 'It's all the digging that's woken it up.'

'It must live in the well after all, like the legend says,' said Moira. 'They only dug up that part of the square last week. Very grateful your mother has arrived, Mary-Kate. A former Wyrm Watch Society member suggested we contact the London Archaeological Society and ask for her.'

'Every bit of research I've ever done points to it living in Round Hill,' said Terry, wiping sweat from his shining forehead.

'This isn't time for fighting about where it sleeps,' said Yolanda firmly. 'What we need to decide is what do we do? This is our chance! It's woken up. How do we get a positive sighting? We need a photo. We all know what Lord Woolington said. The shopping centre proceeds unless there is evidence.'

'Did you see the fence at Green Corner? Something giant smashed it. Why is that not enough proof?' said Graham emphatically.

'Or all that brown slime on the stones?' said Moira.

'Please keep your voices down,' cautioned Yolanda. Brown slime.

Mary-Kate wished she hadn't heard that.

La-la-la-la-la, she said to herself.

Slime that was brown. Brown that was slime. She shuddered and tried to slow her breathing.

Fortunately, Yolanda stood up. In her library, she did not look frightened at all. Although she was tiny, she looked in command. Her cheeks flushed pink as she placed her hands on her hips.

'What we need is a photograph,' she said. 'We all know it! The foundations are poured tomorrow afternoon at five. After that, the well is gone forever. And maybe the wyrm with it. We need proof of its existence beyond legend!'

The small circle applauded. Mary-Kate clapped softly too. Yolanda sat down again.

'I'm going to be really honest here,' said Terry, softly. He looked apologetically at Mary-Kate. 'I'm really scared. If this thing is real, I mean. Remember the children? If it's angry, we could all be at risk.'

'Excuse me, what happened to the children?' asked Mary-Kate. The question was out of her mouth before she could stop it. The small group looked uncomfortable for several seconds.

'The legend says that in 1866, six children were taken by the wyrm over a three-week period,' said Graham. The rest of the group fidgeted nervously as this information was relayed.

'Oh,' said Mary-Kate. 'I see.'

'Then it wasn't seen again until 1934,' he continued. 'And then of course this past Sunday night.'

'And it didn't eat any children in 1934,' said Yolanda, hopefully, 'or on Sunday night. We can't be too careful though, can we?'

'I say we set up a roster for a stake-out tonight,' suggested Moira. 'Someone with a camera at all times, watching from a cottage closest to the square. Who's in?'

'I think it should be in pairs,' stammered Terry. 'No one should have to be alone.'

'Good idea,' said Graham. 'Let me take first shift.

I've a got a really high-powered camera that will work much better at night. We can't rely on mobile phones for this kind of thing. They'll say we've fiddled with the images.'

'I'll draw up the roster,' said Moira, who already had paper and pen in hand. 'Would you like to be on it, Mary-Kate?'

Mary-Kate was about to answer when the door to the village library was flung open abruptly and Lord Woolington stood framed by the sunlight outside.

'Sorry I'm late!' he boomed in his huge friendly voice, raking back his fringe and dragging a chair loudly across the room and into the circle. 'Hello, Graham, I certainly didn't expect to see you here. And Mary-Kate, I'm very sad to see that you've somehow been roped into this.'

Dignified-looking Graham had gone red in the face. He stared at the floor.

But Yolanda leaped up.

'You!' she said. 'You are not welcome here!'

'That's unfriendly,' replied Lord Woolington,

pleasantly. 'I wanted to keep up-to-date on developments. Any more sightings?'

'This is all your fault,' said Moira, standing up too and looking just as fierce as Yolanda. 'You and your shopping centre. You've damaged the well even though you knew it was of historical significance.'

Lord Woolington laughed loudly and then looked at the small circle with something like pity.

'Everything I've done is well within the law. Section 143, paragraph 32, subclause 15 of the local Planning Act: on privately owned land where there is no proof of a legendary creature's actual existence, structures associated with said legendary creatures may be demolished as long as a small plaque is left commemorating their location. In case you have forgotten, Mrs Lewis, I own this land.'

'And we all know who helped write that law,' fumed Ms Honey.

Lord Woolington shook his head and smiled sadly.

'I've attended this emergency meeting because I want to let you all know that dredging up this ridiculous myth will get you nowhere. It's plain to see that the Say No to the Shopping Centre Action Group and the Wyrm Watch Society are really the same thing. Graham, I cannot believe you are involved in this. Most disappointing. The Woolington Shopping Centre will go ahead, no matter what fanciful stories you come up with. You know what the law says. You've known for months. A legend is a legend. Unless you can provide proof of this monster, then the foundations will be poured tomorrow afternoon.'

He used his fingers to make quotation marks in the air as he uttered the word 'monster'.

'We'd like you to leave now, please,' said Ms Honey. Mary-Kate could tell she was trying to make herself look bigger and more intimidating; her chin was raised, but her body was trembling.

Lord Woolington stood slowly. He towered over her.

'The wyrm does not exist,' he said, slowly and calmly.

Then he turned on his heel and left, the library doors banging closed behind him.

Mary-Kate wondered if all meetings were this awkward. There was quiet after Lord Woolington left, Graham staring, stony-faced, at the carpet. Moira muttering 'Section 143' under her breath. Terry wringing his hands. Yolanda took the roster that had been drawn up, and photocopied it on an ancient-looking photocopier in the corner of the library. Mary-Kate was not on it. They'd all looked slightly disappointed when she'd said she'd probably have to ask her mother first if she was allowed to stay up that late.

But Mary-Kate also had questions. Several questions. They were chasing themselves around in her head and she knew she needed her strawberry-scented notebook and the lime-green glitter pen to set them straight. *Was the well that Moira mentioned the well from the legend? Was that where the Professor had been standing in the construction site? Did the wyrm really eat children? Was the wyrm real? How were they going to get a photo of something if it wasn't real?*

'Thanks for attending the meeting,' said Moira, patting her on the shoulder. 'It means the world to us to know there are other believers.'

Mary-Kate smiled politely and chewed on her bottom lip. That was the problem: she didn't know if she *did* believe. Large fire-breathing serpent-like creatures were not the kinds of things that she had ever really thought of. It was strange to be thinking of them right now. She didn't want to say that, though. Instead, she nodded.

What she *did* know was that she felt she should help the members of the Wyrm Watch Society. That was an even stranger feeling because she wasn't sure at all how she could.

She looked around at them. Yolanda turning off the photocopier. Graham slumped in his chair. Terry wiping his forehead with a large handkerchief. Moira had gone to pat Graham on the shoulder too.

'Sorry, Graham,' said Moira. 'Sorry he had to find out like that.'

'Never mind,' replied Graham, lifting himself up dejectedly. 'It was bound to happen sooner or later. I'll return the car and hand in my resignation.'

'Shall we walk you back to the Hook & Wyrm, Terry?' asked Moira. 'Safety in numbers. Mary-Kate, you can come too.'

'I'd like to stay, if that's all right Ms Honey?' said Mary-Kate.

'Please call me Yolanda,' said the librarian.

'I'd like to look in the library and ...'

She couldn't think of how to say it.

There *was* a mystery to be solved here.

A puzzle of sorts.

She needed to find out if the Woolington Wyrm had really reappeared and if it was real. And if it was real then why was it angry and smashing fences and leaving slime? And if it was real, get a photograph of it before five tomorrow afternoon to stop the cement foundations of the Woolington Shopping Centre being poured and the village being changed forever and the oaks on the green being bulldozed.

It seemed too hard to summarise all that. She patted the silver packet in her black dress pocket.

Terry, Graham, Yolanda and Moira waited.

'I would like to help,' said Mary-Kate.

Famous Monster Hunter
Sir Reginald Wavell often said
helpfulness is the most useful trait
a monster hunter can possess.

*P.K. Mayberry's Complete Guide to
Monsters of the Northern Hemisphere*

Mary-Kate wrote in lime-green glitter pen while Yolanda tidied away the circle of chairs. Writing things down was the best way she knew to make sense of things. She wrote quickly in dot points, her glittery letters filling half a page.

* Where does the wyrm really live?
* Has the construction woken up the wyrm?
* Is the wyrm angry?
* Will it eat more children?
* Is the wyrm even real?

She looked at that last question for some time.

Yolanda coughed softly.

'Can I show you something, Mary-Kate?' she asked.

She motioned to Mary-Kate to follow her to the back of the small library to a space behind several bookshelves. There in a little alcove she flipped a light switch. An exhibition blazed to life. An exhibition on the Woolington Wyrm. There were several news cuttings displayed behind glass as well as a map of the village dotted with colourful thumbtacks. There were even some T-shirts in a neat pile. The T-shirts said 'HOME OF THE WOOLINGTON WYRM SINCE 1317'. At the centre of the exhibition there was a large painting of the wyrm in a carved wooden frame.

Mary-Kate looked at the painting of the Woolington Wyrm.

'Oh my,' she said.

The wyrm was enormous. In the painting it was winding its way across the countryside beneath a fiery sky. It had terrible sharp teeth, and long slimy whiskers trailed from its chin. Whoever had painted the wyrm had forgotten to give it eyes and this made Mary-Kate feel worried because it seemed like an important thing to forget. Also, the wyrm was a mixture of colours, but most belonged to the brown family. Mary-Kate searched for another colour and found something that looked like olive. She was grateful for it.

'Yolanda,' she said slowly. 'I'm wondering if you could please tell me everything you know about the wyrm?'

Mary-Kate wrote the words 'IMPORTANT INFORMATION' in large sky-blue glitter letters as Yolanda moved two chairs in front of the exhibition.

'There was once a man by the name of James Woolington,' she began after they were seated. 'Although you'd know that from the newspaper today, wouldn't you?'

'I'm happy to hear everything you have to say,' replied Mary-Kate, pen poised. She needed as much information as possible, she'd decided. A kind of background brief on this creature.

'The year was recorded as 1317. James Woolington went fishing one day and caught a strange creature. It was only a wee thing, like a worm I suppose. He noticed it could breathe out of water. He threw it in the village well, hoping to show his older brothers when they returned from the war in France, but of course they didn't. Nor did half the village men who'd also gone to fight. That same year, when so many in the village mourned the loss of their sons and they were building a stone monument to remember them in the market square, the well dried up and a large serpent-like creature began terrorising the countryside. It appeared at night and ate the sheep grazing in the fields. Word spread that young James Woolington had placed a strange worm in the well months before. They blamed him for the creature that became known as the Woolington Wyrm. They blamed him for the dried-up well, and they even blamed him for the loss of their sons who went to war. It was not a good time to be a Woolington. So, James Woolington found himself a suit of armour and a sword, the first of many young men to do such a thing, and off he went to find this creature and put an end to it. He was never seen again.'

Mary-Kate paused her dot points, thinking. Poor James Woolington, to be blamed for everything.

'The villagers tried everything in those months,' continued Yolanda. 'They tried to board up the top of the well; varying accounts report it was smashed to smithereens. They threw coins into the well and other peace offerings. They even threw in the odd sheep. It did no good. Many brave men went to fight the wyrm. Some accounts told of how they sliced the wyrm with their swords only to find it grow itself together again!'

'Interesting,' said Mary-Kate to encourage her, although, really, she was very upset about the sheep.

'Then one day the wyrm stopped terrifying the town. No one knows why. It simply disappeared. It didn't show up again for nearly two hundred years. This time it was really angry. The year was 1596. We know because work had begun on the Woolington Church. This time the wyrm didn't only like sheep, it also wanted cows.'

Mary-Kate underlined the word 'Cows'.

'The villagers tried something different this time. Word had reached them of another wyrm in another county that had been subdued with milk. The villagers began to leave out pails of milk for the wyrm. And to their surprise, it worked. As long as ample milk was left around the village, the wyrm stayed quiet and eventually disappeared again.'

'The mystery of the milk saucers solved,' said Mary-Kate, and she pumped a fist in the air.

'We thought it was worth a try,' said Yolanda. 'There really aren't many villagers living in Woolington Well anymore. Most of them have left because of the noise and the dust from the construction. We still placed the saucers at every door the way they have done in the past. Back in 1596 the villagers were very pleased and hoped that was it. It wasn't. There are accounts of the wyrm returning in 1672 and again in 1784. And then in 1866, which was a terrible year. This time the milk wasn't working. This time the wyrm had a new taste.'

Mary-Kate changed to the purple glitter pen each time a new date was mentioned so that they stood out. She wished the Woolington Wyrm was purple too, perhaps a lilac colour. She glanced up at the painting. Of course, it wasn't.

She noticed Yolanda Honey had stopped talking.

'Is this the bit where it starts eating children?' asked Mary-Kate.

'So they say. You can see their gravestones in the cemetery. There are six of them. All taken only weeks apart. Not a trace of them was ever found, or so it was said. It must have been a horrible time. Then there is the last official sighting in 1936. That was by a Mrs Madeline Beattie. She saw the wyrm when she was a girl, out walking in the fields near Round Hill. It spurred her on to spend a large part of her life searching for the creature. She lives in the retirement home now.'

'Does she talk about it?' A first-hand witness would probably be very helpful.

'She loves nothing more than to talk about it. She was the founding member of the Wyrm Watch Society. She suggested we apply for the stop work order and send for Professor Martin.'

'Maybe I could visit her?' said Mary-Kate.

'Yes, I'm sure she'd like that very much. Her story goes that she was near the hill and out it came, from the cave there.'

'There's a cave on Round Hill?'

'Yes, there's quite a few caves in the hills around here, limestone after all, but only one on Round Hill. It's called Wyrm Hole. Been explored by experts, doesn't extend very far into the hill at all. Did you know Terry is an experienced potholer? When he first moved to Woolington Well he tried to go further inside the hill, to no avail. He did get a picture one morning though, a very important picture, of some slime near the entrance. We used it in our submission to stop the shopping centre being built, for the protection of the Woolington Wyrm itself. They said it could have been anything. Paint, for instance. Would you like to see it?'

'Maybe I'll look at it later,' stammered Mary-Kate.

'There's also the slime on the fence, out beyond the village green. You should definitely go and take a look at that.'

Mary-Kate hoped the librarian would stop mentioning slime.

'Mrs Lewis got some snaps of the slime on her phone, which she is going to upload to the Wyrm Watch Society website,' continued Yolanda. 'Of course, she has to drive to the next village for that because there's no reception here. I'm not sure, with everything going on, if she's managed it yet. We were going to use them to write another submission for another stop work order in case ...' she trailed off and then, as though only realising it, she clasped Mary-Kate's hands. 'We're running out of time!'

Her last words were spoken in a trembling fashion, as though she was about to cry.

'Don't worry, Yolanda,' said Mary-Kate. She hated to see anyone cry.

'Can I tell you a secret?' said the librarian, breathlessly. 'I looked up to Mrs Beattie so much. She was fearless in her quest to see the wyrm again. Why, she slept up near Round Hill some nights!

She put cameras down the well. She passed over the presidency to me when she retired, even though I had only just turned twenty-one, and I hoped I'd do her proud. And here in the library I'm fine, but now that it has reappeared, I'm terrified.'

'That's perfectly understandable,' said Mary-Kate. She was scared of many things. In fact, things that people were never scared of, like brown colouring-in pencils and mismatched clothing. But for some reason a large child-eating brown wyrm didn't seem to be one of them. She took a deep breath. 'I'm going to help solve this. I really am.'

'Thank you, Mary-Kate,' said Yolanda.

Mary-Kate put her strawberry-scented notebook and glitter pens back in her backpack. She felt full of purpose. If she sat somewhere quiet and read through her dot points, she was sure she would be able to come up with a theory, and a theory was what she needed. She'd never needed a theory before and for some reason this made her smile. She hadn't expected child-eating wyrms or theories on this trip. The mystery of the milk seemed tiny beside what she had to solve.

She looked at the painting of the Woolington Wyrm sliding across the countryside, fire in the sky.

'I'll be back soon,' she said.

She was almost at the door when the floor beneath her feet began to tremble.

The little village library shook violently for several seconds. Shelves wobbled, the photocopier lid chattered, a clock slid down the wall and crashed to the ground. A cart containing books toppled over, causing Yolanda to shriek.

'What on earth?' whispered Mary-Kate when it was over, and stillness had descended.

Absolute silence.

Yolanda had disappeared under a table.

'I think it's stopped. Are you okay?' asked Mary-Kate, bending down to talk to her.

'I forgot to mention the earth tremors,' the librarian whispered.

'Earth tremors?'

'Yes, every so often the earth trembles in Woolington Well. It always has. Geologists say there's a fault line. We say it's the wyrm. There was a large one on Sunday night. Did you know Mrs Lewis keeps a seismometer at the back of her bakery? Should you hide under here with me until we are sure that it's stopped?'

'I think everything is fine, it only lasted a few seconds,' reassured Mary-Kate. 'I have to run to the construction site to make sure my mother is all right.'

'Oh dear, do you think you should?' said Yolanda. 'What if it's out there?'

She was in a state and Mary-Kate knew there was no point trying to reason with her.

'I'm going to leave but first I want you to close your eyes and breathe in through your nose and out through your mouth,' she said calmly.

The librarian did as she was told.

'Slowly,' said Mary-Kate as she backed towards the door. 'In through your nose, out through your mouth. I'll be back soon.'

'Promise?' said Yolanda.

'Promise,' said Mary-Kate. And she opened the door, coming face to face with Lady Arabella Woolington.

'Arabella,' said Mary-Kate.

'Did you feel that?' Arabella had a huge grin on her face. 'The ground was shaking. I love it when that happens.'

She seemed completely unconcerned. She was still wearing her pony-riding attire, the knees of her jodhpurs filthy, her hair in disarray.

'What are you doing here?' asked Mary-Kate.

'I was returning my library books,' said Arabella. She had two books in her hands. 'I've left Pickles tethered on the green.'

'I have to run to the square to see if the tremor came from there,' said Mary-Kate.

'I can show you a short cut,' said Arabella.

She motioned Mary-Kate down the side of the village library and into a small backyard. She pushed open a rickety gate.

'This way,' she said, rushing ahead through a tiny lane that ran between the stone cottages, 'and now over here.'

This time she shimmied over a stone fence and into a vegetable patch.

'Don't step on Ms Penny's lettuces, whatever you do,' she called back as she cleared the next fence like a hurdler. Mary-Kate picked her way through the vegetable patch in her red sparkly shoes. Arabella took her hand to help her from the wall.

'Tada!' She pointed to the village square.

Mary-Kate was relieved to see her mother standing with the construction crew. She was safe!

'Prof,' she called. Her mother looked up and smiled.

'All good,' called her mother, picking her way through the rubble towards Mary-Kate. The small group of construction workers, two women and a man, accompanied her. They looked almost as nervous as Terry had at the Hook & Wyrm. 'Just a slight tremor. Did you feel it? Apparently it's quite common around here.'

'It shook the library,' said Mary-Kate.

'I felt it too,' said Arabella, not to be outdone.

'It's the wyrm for sure,' said one of the construction workers, looking around anxiously.

'Don't be silly,' said another, but Mary-Kate noticed she was sweating.

'I wouldn't go down that hole again, Professor,' said the third. 'It was right underneath us, whatever it was.'

'Were you in the well?' cried Arabella.

'I was indeed, or what's left of it. It's been badly damaged. There hasn't been any water in there for centuries. A bit to be found at the bottom, though; lots of pottery from various eras and quite a few bones.' She pointed to a small collection of items laid out on a sheet nearby. 'There's a small entrance to some kind of subterranean tunnel that has collapsed during the damage. Probably where the underground water source once was. I'll have to call my colleagues in London to confirm how I'll proceed.'

'Oh, the boss isn't going to like this,' said the first construction worker.

Professor Martin nodded.

'I suggest you pack up for the day,' she said. 'Work is indefinitely suspended on the Woolington Shopping Centre until we sort out what's down here.'

When they had retreated, Professor Martin turned to Mary-Kate again.

'How is your mystery solving going?'

Mary-Kate glanced shyly at Arabella.

'Would you excuse us for one minute, Arabella?' said Professor Martin and walked with Mary-Kate a few steps away. 'You look worried. Tell me what you've got so far.'

'Well, I've got a large fire-breathing serpent-like creature that's been around for centuries, and the Wyrm Watch Society want proof of it – a photograph – otherwise the concrete foundations will be poured and the well will be gone forever, that well right there, and maybe the wyrm too,' whispered Mary-Kate. Professor Martin pushed her glasses back up her nose, listening. 'Because some say it lives in the well and some say it lives in Round Hill. Some believe in it and some don't. Lord Woolington definitely doesn't.' She said that last part even quieter, so that Professor Martin had to lean in closer.

'Mostly it doesn't bother anyone,' continued Mary-Kate. 'It disappears for centuries and when it comes back it's usually quite cranky. Eating sheep and cows and knocking over fences. The milk is something the villagers did many centuries ago, to calm it down. It liked it apparently. But the next time it came back it started eating children. That was in 1866.'

Professor Martin's eyes widened at that.

'Did it really?' she muttered. 'What proof do you have?'

'They have headstones in the cemetery.'

Her mother shook her head. 'Maybe there is some misunderstanding here. How can you prove one hundred per cent that it was the wyrm that caused those deaths? Logically, what would you have to do?'

'I'd have to find out more information?' guessed Mary-Kate.

'Yes indeed, good-old fashioned research,' said the Professor. 'There will be a genealogical room in the library, I'm sure. And you could also look at what was going on in Woolington in 1866.'

'And at the other times that it appeared.'

'Yes, I think looking for evidence is where you should start,' said Professor Martin. 'Gathering evidence is the best way to solve any mystery.'

'How do I get a photograph?' asked Mary-Kate.

Professor Martin laughed softly.

'I expect that might be a bit more difficult. We'll dine at six tonight at the Hook & Wyrm and you can tell me what you've come up with,' she said, turning back to Arabella, who was waiting patiently. 'I'm off to phone in details of this find. If I can find some phone coverage, that is. Sorry to keep you waiting, Arabella.'

'There's only reception at Woolington House,' said Arabella. 'We have a satellite dish.'

'Of course,' smiled Professor Martin kindly and Arabella beamed.

'Can I show Mary-Kate around the village?' she asked.

Mary-Kate tried to shoot her mother a glance to tell her that she needed time alone. Time with her strawberry-scented notebook, time to find evidence, time to solve the mystery before five tomorrow afternoon.

But her mother wasn't looking at Mary-Kate. She was looking at Arabella.

'I think that sounds like a wonderful idea, Arabella,' said Professor Martin.

It is a little known, yet useful fact,
that many monster hunters work in pairs.
Sir Reginald Wavell worked with
the brilliant Professor Lavinia Lightfoot.
Mrs Sarah Kite worked with her eldest
son, Lucas. And P.K. Mayberry was always
accompanied by her cat, Mr Tom.

P.K. Mayberry's Complete Guide to
Monsters of the Northern Hemisphere

Mary-Kate and Lady Arabella Woolington walked through the quiet village streets, although there was nothing quiet about Arabella.

'What would you like to see?' she said. 'I can take you anywhere you need to go and if it's far, we could ride on Pickles. I hope he hasn't eaten anything he wasn't meant to. Last time I left him on the green he ate some flowers that had just been planted and I got in dreadful trouble. And once, when I tied him up near the library, he ate Mr Preston's roses over the fence. Mr Preston moved away recently.'

She looked downcast at the last snippet of information, then continued brightly.

'Look what happened to my knees on the way here. I stopped to climb a tree and my foot slipped and I fell. Nothing broken. I'm so glad you felt a tremor. My nanny used to call them the Wyrm Tremblies.'

Arabella grinned at that and then looked downcast again.

'She's in the retirement home now. We could go and visit her perhaps?'

'Wyrm Tremblies?' said Mary-Kate softly. 'You know about the wyrm, don't you?'

'Everyone knows about the legend of the Woolington Wyrm,' said Arabella. 'Is that the mystery you're trying to solve? Maybe I can help. I'm probably really good at mysteries.'

Mary-Kate smiled but she wasn't so sure. Arabella talked so constantly that it hurt Mary-Kate's brain. Mystery solving required notetaking and concentration and quietness.

'Please tell me,' said Arabella. 'I know you don't want to tell me because my father doesn't believe in it and because he likes building shopping centres. It's only, I really …'

Arabella stopped.

'You really what?' asked Mary-Kate. They were at the edge of the green now and there was Pickles on the other side, eating a hedge.

'I really like the wyrm,' said Arabella quietly.

'You believe in it?'

'Yes,' said Arabella, although she looked uncomfortable saying it. She shuffled one boot on the grass, thinking. 'Tell me what you need to solve the mystery. I promise I'll help.'

They sat beneath a large oak at the edge of the village green. The sunlight flickered through the leaves and made Mary-Kate's shoes and backpack sparkle even more. She searched for her notebook and took an extra-long time even though it was right there at her fingertips. What would Arabella think of her clues? She might laugh at them. Like Amelia Blythe-Tompkinson did when Mary-Kate gave a presentation on her international coin collection.

Or something terrible might happen if she showed these pages to Arabella. There might be another earth tremor, only this one would cause an avalanche. The avalanche would cover the entire village. Or …

Or nothing would happen at all. She would take out her notebook and open it. There would simply be her small glitter pen words and perhaps they didn't mean anything at all. Perhaps they were only silly little words. Her heart was beating faster now. She found the lucky globe stress ball and gave it a good squeeze.

'Do you want me to help you find it?' suggested Arabella, helpfully.

'Oh, no, here it is after all,' said Mary-Kate, retrieving the notebook.

You have trouble with beginnings and endings, but you're very good with in-betweens. All she had to do was *start*. She flipped open the notebook and passed it to Arabella who read it slowly, carefully, turning the pages, one by one. Her blue eyes were bright and serious when she looked up.

'So, what do we do next?' she asked.

Mary-Kate felt a pleasant lightness in her body at Arabella's approval of her notebook and her glitter pen words.

'I need to gather evidence,' she said. 'First about the children. Then, well, any evidence at all. I mean, I probably need to write a plan.'

'No time for a plan!' cried Arabella. 'We can find the gravestones at the graveyard, I'm sure. And I've got something very important to show you on the way!'

She jumped up and offered Mary-Kate her hand to pull her up too. Mary-Kate took it, still wishing she could write a plan. Certain things made Mary-Kate feel comforted. Unopened jars of strawberry jam, small puffy clouds, completed bingo cards and infomercials on laundry detergent. And most definitely a plan in the form of a list, written neatly, in dot points.

'I think I should write a quick plan,' said Mary-Kate.

'Write it at the cemetery,' said Arabella Woolington and she was already off and running across the green.

The Very Important Thing was not actually on the way, Mary-Kate discovered. It was in completely the opposite direction to the Woolington Church and graveyard. This minor fact did nothing to dent Arabella's enthusiasm for what she wanted to show Mary-Kate. Arabella ran towards the small bridge that Mary-Kate and her mother had crossed that very morning, then veered at the last minute down towards the stream itself.

'It's on the other side. This way is much quicker than the road,' she called back to Mary-Kate. 'Are you good at rock-hopping?'

Mary-Kate chewed on her bottom lip. Jumping and hopping were not things that she normally did.

'I'm sure you are.' Arabella smiled. She was standing by the edge of the shallow stream, the water rushing over the stones. 'Take your shoes off.'

This made Mary-Kate feel very worried. She would

be completely unbalanced if she took off her shoes. She would be only one quarter sparkle.

'Or,' Arabella suggested hastily, 'imagine your red sparkling shoes have a special rock-hopping magic in them!'

Mary-Kate had never met anyone quite like little mud-stained Lady Arabella Woolington. There were four large rocks across the stream, and Arabella showed her how to jump to the first one. She repeated her demonstration three more times, shouting instructions as she did so.

On the other side of the stream, all four rocks successfully hopped, and her sparkly shoes still dry, Mary-Kate clambered up a sloping field after Arabella and then around a stand of trees. Across the field, Woolington House stood stark and grey and behind it rose Round Hill.

'Oh,' said Arabella, her shoulders slumped. There was a man carrying a bucket near a demolished section of stone fence, stones stacked in piles. 'Mr Blair, what happened to the slime?'

'Hello Lady Arabella,' said Mr Blair, waving and walking towards them. He was an older man with a kind face and a beanie pulled down over his ears. A look of concern crossed his face. 'Lord Woolington wanted it tidied up. Sent me here himself. And I'll come tomorrow to put it all back together, so the sheep don't get out. Going to use some tin sheeting until then. It was a brand-new fence and all. Only went up a couple of weeks ago.'

Arabella didn't look impressed.

'This is the fence the wyrm went through,' she said, turning to Mary-Kate. 'This morning it was covered in brown goo. I rode down on Pickles as soon as I heard. I was going to show you and it's all ruined.'

'Lady Arabella, you can't deny the fence belongs to your father and so does this field, and most fields around here too. And you know he doesn't like talk of the wyrm,' said Mr Blair. 'Best you run along with your little friend and not think about it.'

Mary-Kate was secretly glad there was no slime, especially brown slime. She stared at the large section of fence that had been destroyed. Whatever had crashed through the stone was very big. As wide as a car, at least. She shivered.

'Off you go,' said Mr Blair, kindly. 'Play while there's still sun in the day.'

Arabella high-jumped several fences on the way back to the village. Unnecessarily, Mary-Kate thought, but in doing so she seemed to burn off some of her disappointment. She was her usual cheery self again when they arrived at the small cemetery behind the Woolington Church, which was filled with tumbledown headstones covered in moss beneath large shady yew trees. It took Mary-Kate a minute to catch her breath.

'Here it is,' said Arabella, not out of breath at all. 'Now, to find the headstones. Let's split up. You start with this section and I'll start over near the fence.'

Before Mary-Kate could agree, Arabella was jogging to her starting point and giving a cheery wave when she arrived there. Mary-Kate waved back half-heartedly.

They walked up and down the rows of headstones, Mary-Kate slowly, Arabella briskly, reading the inscriptions. Arabella had finished all the rows before Mary-Kate reached the end of the first. She hadn't found any inscriptions that matched the year 1866.

'I'm sure they're here somewhere,' said Arabella.

'Did you read them all carefully?' asked Mary-Kate.

'I did. I read very fast,' said Arabella, looking a little put-out. 'I'll look again.'

'What about those over there?' Mary-Kate pointed to a heavily shaded section of the graveyard, where

there was a large stone angel with flowing wings
on top of a tombstone.

'I don't really like to go over there,' said Arabella,
glancing in the direction of the angel briefly, and
then looking at the ground.

'That's all right, I'll look,' said Mary-Kate kindly,
although she thought it strange as she set off
to the secluded area. The cemetery was tranquil,
the shadows of the great trees moving over the
headstones, the wind hushing the long grass.

Straightaway, she found the headstones of the six
children who died in 1866. They were in the same

row, all of them, one after another. Had Arabella not wanted her to find them?

'They're here,' she called to Arabella, who was looking at a yew tree intently, as though deciding if she should climb it. 'Come and see.'

Arabella came reluctantly.

Their names were Thomas Glover, Mary Jones, Fred Tanner, Luke Bartholomew, and Gertie and Annie White. Those last two were on the same headstone and it made Mary-Kate let out a whoosh of air.

Their names, birth and death dates appeared on their headstones. They were all young, between two and seven years old. There was no mention of them being eaten by the Woolington Wyrm, and Mary-Kate thought maybe that wasn't something that anyone wanted to add.

She sat down on the grass and chose the most solemn glitter pen colour she could find, which was forest green. She opened her notebook and began to write down the names and the dates carefully.

'It's really sad, isn't it?' said Arabella.

'Yes,' said Mary-Kate.

'I'll read them out so you can write them down,' offered Arabella, sitting down beside her. She recited the names and dates for Mary-Kate, who thanked her. They sat in silence for a while, the dappled light shifting and swaying over them.

'What do we do with this evidence?' asked Arabella, moving closer and peering at Mary-Kate's neat notes.

'We go to the library and research them in the genealogy section,' said Mary-Kate. 'And research the year 1866 too. And then do more research and hope that a theory arrives.'

'A theory,' said Arabella, looking at Mary-Kate with admiration.

'Yes, I'm not really sure how to do them,' said Mary-Kate honestly. 'But I'm going to try.'

They stood up to leave, Mary-Kate placing her pen and notebook away.

'Goodbye,' she said to the headstones. It seemed the right thing to do.

She noticed Arabella had glanced again at the tomb not far from where they stood, the large stone angel with ornate wings towering above the other graves. Mary-Kate glimpsed some of the letters carved on the stone now they were closer, a 'W' and 'O' and another 'O'.

'Woolington?' she whispered. She saw there were many names written on the stone beneath the angel, Woolington after Woolington, lords and ladies, over the centuries. The first dates were barely legible – they had been worn smooth by time – but the more recent dates were etched clearly on the dark stone, the last catching her eye.

LADY ASTRID MARGARET WOOLINGTON – 1984~2019

That wasn't so long ago. She turned to ask Arabella about it, but she was no longer nearby. She'd raced through the headstones and was already waiting at the graveyard gate, her arms crossed, staring in the other direction.

'Hurry up,' she called, not looking at Mary-Kate

or the stone angel. 'Let's go to the library, we've got research to do!'

When they returned to the library, Mary-Kate was glad to see that Yolanda Honey was no longer hiding under the table. Instead she was working at a computer, her fingers tapping quickly. When she looked up, she had a sparkling determination in her eyes.

'I'm sure you heard from your mother, Mary-Kate, that work is halted until more experts arrive from London in the morning?' She smiled. 'It gives us time to prepare another stop work order to halt the foundations being poured and the well being destroyed forever. Moira will submit it first thing in the morning, along with any photos we secure tonight.'

'That's good news,' said Mary-Kate, noticing that Arabella was hiding behind her. Yolanda could see her, of course.

'Have you brought the overdue books with you, Arabella?' asked the librarian, kindly.

'Hello, Yolanda,' said Arabella sheepishly, stepping out from behind Mary-Kate. 'I accidentally left them in Pickles's saddlebag.'

'Arabella is helping me learn about the village,' said Mary-Kate quickly. 'We'd like to use the genealogy room please, and the local history section.'

'Genealogy?' said Yolanda, surprised. 'Right this way.'

She stood up and ushered them briskly to a small room close to the alcove containing the wyrm exhibition. Mary-Kate caught a glimpse of the creature winding its way across the fields, and thought of the stone fence lying in pieces.

'We have digitalised parish records on this computer here, including birth and death records,' said Yolanda. 'Fortunately, you don't need an internet connection for it. I hope it all still works. No one has used it for some time.'

She wiped some dust from the top of the monitor. When the screen came to life, she showed Mary-

Kate and Arabella how to perform a name search.

'We also have issues of the *Woolington Warbler* dated back until ... let me see ... the 1850s. They have been scanned into this file.'

She pointed to an icon on the screen.

'I'm afraid you can only search by date, though. And the local history books are in that row there,' she continued, pointing to shelves nearby. 'Good luck.'

Mary-Kate and Arabella pressed two chairs close together in front of the screen once Yolanda was gone. Mary-Kate opened her notebook and passed it to Arabella, who read out the first name.

'Thomas Glover, 1864–1866,' she said as Mary-Kate typed.

'He was so little,' said Mary-Kate sadly, as a scanned document popped up. It was the death record of poor little Thomas Glover. 'Death cause: diphtheria.'

Arabella and Mary-Kate looked at each other.

'Try this one,' said Arabella in a hushed voice. 'Fred Tanner 1860–1866.'

Mary-Kate typed and they both leaned forwards as the file popped up.

'Diphtheria!' cried Arabella. 'What even is that?'

'A disease,' said Mary-Kate. 'I think. Should we look at 1866 in the *Woolington Warbler*? Maybe there's a headline about it.'

She clicked on the icon that the librarian had pointed out. She scrolled slowly through the scanned pages. 1866 had been a busy year in Woolington Well.

First, there was: `WOOLINGTON INN FIRE`

The inn, situated on the market square, had caught fire one night in March and was so badly damaged that it needed to be demolished. Work began to rebuild it not long after. After that there were three large earth tremors, a landslide at Round Hill and several sheep stolen. All these events were believed to be the work of the Woolington Wyrm. The headlines trumpeted:

`THE WOOLINGTON WYRM RETURNS`

`BEWARE THE WOOLINGTON WYRM`

`WOOLINGTON WYRM AWAKENS`

'Mysterious,' said Mary-Kate. She felt there was a theory starting to form, a wispy, floaty theory, which she couldn't quite catch.

There was no mention of the wyrm eating children, though.

'Keep scrolling,' said Arabella after Mary-Kate jotted down these events in her notebook.

They both gasped when the next slid into view: DIPHTHERIA DEATHS. It was a story about the deaths of many children, and no one was blaming the wyrm. Arabella read the article aloud, describing the terrible illness that ravaged the village. The article mentioned the names of three children: Thomas Glover, Mary Jones and Fred Tanner. She scrolled further and found the death notices of three more children: Luke Bartholomew, and Gertie and Annie White.

'Poor children,' whispered Mary-Kate.

'Why?' said Arabella. 'Why would someone make up that story about the wyrm?'

'Maybe because it was such a horrible, sad thing to

happen, they had to make up a story about it?' suggested Mary-Kate. 'It was the only way of coping with it.'

'You still believe in the wyrm, don't you?' said Arabella. 'I mean, even if it didn't take the children, what about all the other things?'

She looked at Mary-Kate anxiously.

'I like facts,' said Mary-Kate, honestly. 'We've disproved one story about the wyrm, but I guess that doesn't mean it's definitely not real.'

Arabella gripped her arm. She was very upset.

'I know it's real because—' she started to say before they heard the library door open.

'Good afternoon again, Ms Honey,' a voice boomed. It was Lord Woolington. 'You are no doubt feeling very happy that work has been halted at the construction site until tomorrow!'

Mary-Kate stood up and moved to the bookshelves, peering through a gap. Lord Woolington had a smile on his face, yet something told Mary-Kate he was anything but happy.

'It's brilliant news,' said the young librarian in an

equally forced cheery tone. 'That well should never have been destroyed.'

'Five tomorrow afternoon, this will all be cleared up by then,' he countered.

'Are you looking for Arabella?' replied Ms Honey, coolly. 'She's in the genealogy room.'

Mary-Kate sat back down and quickly minimised the screen.

'Hello, Papa,' said Arabella when Lord Woolington walked into the room.

'Hello! What are you two up to?' He glanced at the screen.

'Mary-Kate was showing me some archaeological things on a website,' lied Arabella, jumping up. 'Do I have to come home? Can't I stay a little longer?'

'Unfortunately no, dear, we have dinner guests,' said Lord Woolington, nodding to Mary-Kate. 'I'm sure you'll see Mary-Kate tomorrow. Maybe she and the Professor will stay to watch the foundations be poured.'

Arabella smiled sadly at Mary-Kate.

'See you in the morning, I hope,' she said, then

followed her father from the library.

Mary-Kate sat in the silence for some time. It seemed very quiet without Arabella Woolington. She would never have thought when she'd set out that morning on the train that not only would she be researching a large fire-breathing wyrm, but that she'd also make a friend. She was starting to enjoy having someone help her to solve a mystery.

She picked up her notebook from the table. She had work to do. She'd be able to tell Arabella what she'd discovered when she saw her in the morning. For now, she had to catch that theory that was fluttering in her head. Her plan was to cross-reference every wyrm appearance in her notebook with headlines in the *Woolington Warbler*. She was going to write that plan down in large glittery dot points.

She stared at the open page.

Arabella had written something.

She'd written it in purple glitter pen. She'd written

it in messy handwriting. It must have been when they'd heard Lord Woolington enter while Mary-Kate had been standing near the bookshelves.

Arabella Woolington had written,

I know the wyrm is REAL, because I've seen it.

Truth is at the heart of every
monster hunter's search.

*P.K. Mayberry's Complete Guide to
Monsters of the Northern Hemisphere*

Mary-Kate knew she should be focused on the words themselves. Not the fact that they were messy. Not that they were written in her notebook. Not that they were written on a page that she couldn't rip out because it had other important information on it. *Don't be silly*, she told herself, but that only made it worse.

That awful scrawl in her notebook made Mary-Kate feel like something terrible was about to happen. Perhaps another earth tremor, only this one would be huge. The whole village would collapse into a sinkhole. She would be left clinging to the sides, which would be mossy, slippery. Down below there would be smashed-up village, stone and thatch and ...

She slammed her notebook shut. Extracted her stress ball.

She sat for a minute squeezing rhythmically as she breathed.

She opened the book again.

She drew a raspberry glitter pen frame around Arabella's words. It was a neat frame with some curled decorations at the corners. She added some lime-green swirls because they were complementary colours. Finally, beneath the frame she wrote neatly and carefully.

Important Witness Evidence.
Interview to follow.

She breathed a sigh of relief that it was sorted.

She could look at Arabella's words now. What did she mean – she'd seen it? Had she really seen it? Or actually been near it?

'Is everything all right, Mary-Kate?' asked Yolanda. She'd arrived with tea and biscuits. 'I thought you might be hungry.'

Mary-Kate turned the page quickly and smiled. She was about to tell her about the children in 1866; how the wyrm couldn't be blamed for it. Something stopped her though. Yolanda desperately wanted the wyrm to be real and maybe she wouldn't like to have this fact disproven. Like the way Arabella had gripped her arm. Mary-Kate sensed that the wyrm meant something different to everyone and that they felt passionately about it, whether they believed or not.

'I'm going to try to do some cross-checking of the dates you gave me earlier,' said Mary-Kate. 'The newspaper only goes back as far as the 1850s, doesn't it?'

'I think this book might be useful,' said Yolanda, running her fingers along a row of books on the nearest shelf. '*The Complete History of the Parish of Woolington Well*. For the earlier dates, at least. Would you like me to help? We have an hour until closing time.'

'Thank you,' said Mary-Kate.

She crunched on her biscuit, her pen poised, as Yolanda took a seat before the computer. Mary-Kate had left two whole pages for the interview with Arabella and she'd transcribed the dates of the wyrm appearances from earlier pages with spaces in-between for any information they found. The title for this new set of dot points was rather long although also strangely satisfying.

THINGS THAT HAPPENED IN THE SAME YEAR THE WYRM CAUSED TROUBLE.

She used her deep-blue glitter pen.

'Okay. Working forwards or backwards?' asked Yolanda.

'Forwards, please,' said Mary-Kate, because backwards reminded her of the idea of facing backwards on a train.

The first date she'd written was 1317. This was the year that James Woolington had placed the strange creature in the well. She knew there had been a war in France and that many of the village men had not returned. A monument was being built to honour them in the market square. She wrote 'War' and 'Monument being built in market square' beside this date.

The next date was 1596.

Yolanda opened the book she had taken from the shelf. It was an old book, leather bound, much like the ones Mary-Kate had seen in the hotel room.

'Something that happened around 1596 in Woolington, you say?' said the librarian. 'Here it is. Remember, I told you, a new church was being built right beside the market square? The old church had burned down. This new church was quite grand and took almost ten years to build.'

That is interesting, thought Mary-Kate. She wrote down the dates '1596 to 1606'. She remembered Yolanda saying that the wyrm had caused problems for many years around these dates.

'What about around 1672?' asked Mary-Kate as Yolanda turned the pages.

'In 1670, construction began on the new village hall,' she read. 'It's the grand old building to the east of the square. You probably didn't notice it with all the scaffolding. Does that help?'

'Does it say how long it took?'

'Here, it says construction took almost five years,' said Yolanda.

Even more interesting, thought Mary-Kate.

'What about 1783?'

'Let me see,' said Yolanda. 'Hmm. In 1780, the Woolington Church burned down again.'

'Yes!' said Mary-Kate, excitedly, and then felt bad because she shouldn't be happy about anything burning down. Yolanda was looking at her quizzically.

'There's a pattern emerging, you see,' said Mary-Kate. 'Did they build another church?'

'They did except not there, they built it where the church stands today. In the place where the church burned to the ground, a large tavern called the Woolington Inn was built. It says construction started in 1783.'

That only left 1866 and 1936.

Mary-Kate knew from previously searching 1866 that the Woolington Inn near the square had burned down and been rebuilt and that there had been earth tremors and a landslip at Round Hill. She wrote these down beneath the date.

'What about 1936?' she asked tentatively, crossing her fingers on both hands.

Yolanda turned to the *Woolington Warbler* files. She scrolled quickly to that year and searched through the pages.

'What about a new roof and restoration of the village hall?' she said. 'Oh, and the square was dug up and new pipes laid because of recent flooding.'

'Bingo!' shouted Mary-Kate and then clamped her hand over her mouth. It was against the rules to shout in libraries. 'Sorry.'

'That's quite all right,' said Yolanda. She looked confused as to what Mary-Kate had discovered.

'Here, I'll show you,' said Mary-Kate, turning her notebook. 'All the dates when there have been reports about the wyrm, on the same dates or around them, there is always something happening in the market square. Always. Big things. Maybe the well is covered over in these times or there is a lot of noise. There would surely be a big racket if a whole church was being built, right? Maybe the wyrm doesn't like things happening near the well?'

'I see what you mean,' said Yolanda, thoughtfully. 'And at the moment the square is completely dug up. And the section where the well stands was only broken apart last week, despite us saying it was important!'

'Every time the wyrm appears, there is something big happening in the square,' said Mary-Kate softly again. 'Maybe it doesn't like people messing with its well?'

She had disproved the story of the wyrm eating children and proved that wyrm rampages were always associated with disruption to the square, but none of this really helped her completely prove the wyrm's existence.

'I better close up,' said Yolanda, interrupting her thoughts. 'I'm first shift with Graham for wyrm watch patrol.'

'Thank you for helping me,' said Mary-Kate.

'I think I'm getting there.'

And though Yolanda smiled kindly, Mary-Kate knew what she was really thinking. They were running out of time.

Mary-Kate sank into her four-poster bed at the Hook & Wyrm Inn, a flutter of nerves in her belly. Would the wyrm return again now that the sun was setting? There had been an air of excitement among the Wyrm Watch Society members as they walked Mary-Kate back to the Hook & Wyrm Inn. Graham had been carrying the large expensive camera he'd spoken of, and his earlier despondency seemed to have lifted. Moira had obtained keys to a cottage on the square that she kept tidy for one of the villagers who'd vacated until the shopping centre building was completed. Yolanda, while glancing from side to side as though the wyrm might appear at any minute, had also been smiling. Mary-Kate thought they looked like three nervous children going to a birthday party.

'The Wyrm Watch Society is going to stay up all night and try to get a photo of the wyrm, Prof,' she said.

Her mother was changing for dinner. Another set of tan pants and a sensible bone-coloured shirt.

'Good luck to them,' she said.

Mary-Kate had told Professor Martin about the events of the afternoon. She hadn't been able to wait until dinner. She'd described the smashed wall straightaway, as soon as she was in the hotel room, and how it was being cleaned up by one of Lord Woolington's employees. She described how she and Arabella had visited the cemetery, and mentioned the name and date she'd seen at the bottom of the Woolington family grave. She explained how they'd completely disproved the story of the wyrm taking children, how it was diphtheria instead, and how they'd made a connection between wyrm appearances and construction in the square.

'Mary-Kate, you have been very busy!' said Professor Martin.

From the hotel room windows, Mary-Kate saw the sun was dipping down behind Round Hill and turning the fields golden. Woolington House stood dark and lonely in the distance and Mary-Kate thought of Arabella there.

'What do you make of it all, Prof?' Her eyes drifted to the tapestry of Woolington House, the figure fishing from the bridge in the foreground. 'Is it ...'

She stopped, closed her eyes. She was missing something. Something important.

'Is it what?' asked Professor Martin, coming to stand beside her and stroking her forehead.

Mary-Kate had been going to say, *is it real*? But she didn't want to say that. She thought of Arabella clutching her arm. Of the young librarian hiding beneath the table. Of the stone wall lying in pieces. Of the creature in the painting, the wild angry-looking creature, which gobbled up livestock and young men with swords. Why did she want it to be real? For that's what she'd realised right then. She wanted it to be real. She *desperately* wanted it to be real.

So that she could help it.

Because, even though she had absolutely no evidence to support the claim, she was almost entirely certain that the wyrm needed help.

'Nothing.' Mary-Kate smiled at her mother. 'Just trying to work things out.'

'Remember what Granny always says, Mary-Kate?' said Professor Martin. 'Sometimes you need to eat and sleep on it.'

Mary-Kate ate well in the cosy dining room, a delicious meal of fish and chips, prepared by

Terry himself who was cook as well as concierge. 'No staff anymore,' he apologised, 'not since the construction began. No visitors either, to tell the truth.'

'It's very tasty,' said Mary-Kate, encouragingly.

Terry still looked nervous. Mary-Kate watched him tidy up as she and her mother played a game of draughts by the fire. He glanced at the windows as he wiped the table and swept the front foyer. Eventually he took his hat and scarf from a hook.

'Will that be all for tonight, Professor Martin?' he asked. 'I've got somewhere that I'm meant to be.'

'Yes, thank you very much,' said Professor Martin.

'Good luck,' said Mary-Kate softly and Terry nodded.

Sometimes you need to eat and sleep on it.

Mary-Kate had eaten but she doubted she could ever sleep. She prowled the hotel suite, peering through windows. She wore her sky-blue Japanese pyjamas with her matching slippers.

They made a satisfying shushing noise on the wooden floor. A moon rode high in the sky, bathing the empty streets below. Woolington House in the distance was in darkness. She wished there was a way to contact Arabella. She wanted to tell her she'd interview her in the morning; she'd listen to everything that she had to say. She'd left some pages blank in the notebook.

'Mary-Kate, I think you need to try to lie down and sleep,' said Professor Martin, drawing the curtains shut.

Mary-Kate tried. She lay on her huge bed thinking thoughts of sleeping. No sleep came. She sat up, unzipped her backpack and took out her Big Ben-shaped novelty torch. She shone it on a page of the notebook and chose a glitter pen, this one cherry red. **The Plan for Tomorrow**, she wrote.

* Meet Arabella and hear her story
* Find out if the WWS got a photo of the wyrm

* Visit Mrs Beattie in the retirement home

She sat for a long time; she didn't want to write the last point.

* Research worm-like creatures

She was certain that to understand the wyrm she needed to know more about it. About its body. About its movements. About its … slime.

She closed the book quickly, crept from the bed to the window. She looked down at the empty, still streets below and across the fields to Woolington House. She raised her lucky Big Ben torch. The torch had been given to her when she was small, by her granny who liked unusual things. Salt and pepper shakers shaped like cats or egg cups shaped like cars. Nearly everything her granny gave her, Mary-Kate considered lucky. She wondered what Granny would make of Woolington Well.

Mary-Kate aimed the torch at Woolington House and flashed once, paused, flashed again.

The windows stayed dark.

What did Arabella mean? *The wyrm is real. I've seen it.*

She tried the torch again. Flash, pause, flash. There was no reply. Her silk pyjama-clad shoulders slumped. She pressed her forehead to the glass. *It will be fine*, she told herself, *you'll see Arabella in the morning.*

A tiny light appeared in one of the top windows of Woolington House. Mary-Kate gasped with delight, then covered her mouth. She didn't want to wake her mother.

She flashed back. Three times.

Three flashes were returned, making her smile.

She waved even though she knew she couldn't be seen from that distance. She waved and whispered, 'See you in the morning.'

She turned off her lucky Big Ben torch and climbed back into bed. Her body was suddenly heavy with weariness. She turned on her side, her eyes already closing. *Eat and sleep on it*, she imagined her granny saying. And she did. She drifted down, down, down, into dreams where she searched with her lucky Big Ben torch through tunnels and sent Morse Code across oceans and opened books filled with theories, and it wasn't until the moon had disappeared below the horizon and the streets were in darkness, that the screaming began.

It is important to remember
that monsters bring out a
range of emotions in humans.

*P.K. Mayberry's Complete Guide to
Monsters of the Northern Hemisphere*

'What on earth?' Professor Martin leaped out of bed and into her dressing-gown. Mary-Kate sat upright, a hand over her thumping heart. There was another loud bellow from somewhere in the village followed by what sounded like the rumbling of rocks. The walls of the Hook & Wyrm Inn trembled ever so slightly.

'Quickly, Mary-Kate,' said Professor Martin, 'look out that window.'

She pointed to the window closest to Mary-Kate's bed. She herself raced to the window on the opposite side of the suite and pulled back the curtain.

Mary-Kate drew the drapes with shaking hands.

There was another noise now. A huge noise.

A wild, angry screeching noise. It rattled the walls. It echoed in her ears.

Her eyes darted down to the street. Nothing.

She glanced at the distant fields. Nothing. She heard her mother behind her make a small, astonished noise. A tiny gasp.

'Over here!' said Professor Martin, and Mary-Kate raced across the suite, tripping in her silk slippers, righting herself again.

'What was it? What did you see? Was it the wyrm?' cried Mary-Kate, looking down at the street below. It was eerily still. The screeching had been replaced by silence. The rumbling had stopped. There was no more shouting.

'It may have been my eyes playing tricks on me,' said Professor Martin. 'But I saw a very big shadow on the walls of those cottages and when I looked down to the street ... well, something was moving fast, I couldn't quite catch it. It was gone in a blink.'

'The wyrm,' whispered Mary-Kate, gazing down into the street.

Figures had emerged now from the darkness. There was tiny Yolanda creeping from behind a cottage and beside her Graham, holding his camera.

Moira came running from another lane.

'Let's go down and see if they're okay,' said Professor Martin, rushing towards the door.

They raced down the stairs into the foyer and found Terry huddled behind the front desk, despite the frantic knocking at the inn's front door. He seemed frozen with fear. The Professor went to help him, placing a comforting hand on his shoulder, while Mary-Kate unlocked the large wooden door. The three Wyrm Watch Society members tumbled into the inn, shocked expressions on their faces. Moira was wet through, as though she'd gone for a swim in the stream. She was also nursing an injured arm.

'We saw it! Or part of it, anyway,' whispered Yolanda, her face pale. 'It was enormous. Magnificent.'

'The most incredible thing I've ever seen,' stammered Graham, the camera shaking in his hands.

'Please tell me you got a photo of it, Graham?' asked Moira.

'Was it the wyrm?' asked Terry, who had been helped to a chair in the lounge.

Yolanda was staring into space as though remembering it.

'Yes,' said Graham, taking the seat opposite Terry. The others gathered around, including Mary-Kate. She noticed Moira was dripping onto the floor. 'We were both nearly asleep, slumped at the windowsill, when we heard a sound. A low sound, a kind of dragging sound and then ...'

He stopped, quivered all over, while Yolanda took over.

'We saw its tail,' she said. 'It was sliding right past our window. I'm sure it was its tail. And then it ...'

'Screeched,' said Moira. 'I heard it and I ran out the front door of the bakery, but it was already gone. I slipped over in some of the slime it had left behind and fell onto my arm.'

'Oh dear, let me take a look at that,' said Professor Martin, motioning to Moira's arm. 'That looks nasty. Mary-Kate, please rush upstairs and grab some towels. And perhaps we can use that small tablecloth over there to fashion a sling.'

Professor Martin was always unwaveringly practical.

'I'll fetch it,' said Terry, who seemed to have unfrozen. He stood up and retrieved the tablecloth while Mary-Kate took the stairs two at a time. She didn't want to miss a single snippet of the conversation.

It was true, then. It was true! They had proof! They'd seen the wyrm. Or at least they'd seen the tail. The shopping centre would be stopped and … She couldn't wait to tell Arabella. But why was it angry? It must be the damage to its well! That had to be it. These thoughts raced around her head, repeating and echoing as she flew back down the stairs, the towels and a blanket in her hands.

Professor Martin had placed Moira's arm in a sling and Mary-Kate handed her the towel. Now that she was close to Moira, Mary-Kate noticed that she wasn't so much wet as coated in a jelly-like substance.

A distinctively brown jelly-like substance. Mary-Kate shuddered. *Best not look*, she told herself, and focused on her mother wrapping the blanket around Moira.

'Oh, I wish I'd seen it,' Moira was saying, her body shaking as shock took over. 'I can't wait to see the photos, Graham.'

Graham smiled. He had the large camera still clutched in both his hands.

'I started clicking as soon as we heard the sound. Everything we need is on the film inside here,' he said. 'I'm going home immediately to the dark room to start developing them.'

He flicked open the back of the camera to extract the canister of film. Mary-Kate had seen film before because her granny used it for her bus trips. She refused to use newfangled things like smart phones and digital cameras.

Graham went silent and a strange expression took over his face. A type of sadness. A terrible, shocked sadness. His mouth hung open.

'The film,' he gasped. 'There's no film in here!'

Sir Reginald Wavell always said that
besides helpfulness, good old-fashioned
determination is a most useful weapon.

*P.K. Mayberry's Complete Guide
to Monsters of the Northern Hemisphere*

Mary-Kate placed the lucky silver packet containing the last seven pieces of gum her father had left behind into her navy-blue dress pocket. She had accessorised again with her sparkly red shoes and sparkly red backpack, and pinned a small navy bow above her fringe. She was glad she was the correct proportions of colour and sparkle.

She needed to feel calm because she had a lot to do. She had squeezed the most important thing that she had to do into the top of the plan she'd written yesterday. She wrote it in bright lemon-coloured glitter pen and circled it three times.

✳ Get a photo of the Woolington Wyrm

She didn't know how she was going to do this, but she knew it was what she must do if she was going to help it. And again, she was now almost certain that the wyrm needed help.

The dejected members of the Wyrm Watch Society had departed in the first dawn light. Graham went hastily first. He had been unable to make eye contact with any of his Wyrm Watch colleagues after he'd discovered there was no film in his camera. Yolanda Honey was next, wiping her eyes, which were red from crying, and finally Moira, accompanied by Terry, departed for the nearest clinic at Lessington to have her arm seen to.

Professor Martin clicked the hotel door shut behind them.

'Well,' said Professor Martin, 'let's have tea and toast in the room and then get our day started. My colleagues will be here by no later than nine, I'd say.'

Arabella was waiting on the inn's front step when they came downstairs again. Pickles was eating the snow peas that had grown over the inn fence.

'Mary-Kate!' shouted Arabella, jumping up and lifting Mary-Kate from the ground with the force of her hug.

'Hello,' said Mary-Kate, who wasn't used to that sort of thing. She smoothed down her dress. Professor Martin smiled.

'Did you see the slime all down the street? Papa says they're going to clean it with a firehose soon. You can still see it. Usually it fades really quick in the sun. He says it's fake. I saw your torch. That was you, wasn't it? I had to go all the way to the kitchen to get a torch and then I realised I could have just turned my lamp on and off.'

Lady Arabella Woolington was in full flight. She wore the same clothes as yesterday, the same mud stains on her knees and riding helmet slipping off one side of her golden frizz.

'Did you hear that the Wyrm Watch Society didn't get a photo after all?' she continued. 'Where are we going this morning? What's the first thing we have to do?'

'First, let's go somewhere quiet and look at the notebook,' said Mary-Kate. 'The village green, maybe? I have things to ask you.'

She looked to her mother to check if that was okay.

'Of course. Off you go, you pair. Good luck. I'm going to the square to wait for the team. Shall we meet back here for a late lunch? Maybe at two?'

Pickles didn't want to leave his meal of sweet peas. Eventually Arabella was able to persuade him with a half-eaten piece of carrot that she fished from her back pocket. It was always important to have carrot or apple available when dealing with Pickles, Arabella explained, because he was a very stubborn pony. She led him down the street, his hooves clopping loudly on the cobblestones, feeding him the carrot intermittently.

'Look, there's some!' she cried, pointing out a wet, sticky substance on the stone. 'See it?'

Mary-Kate stepped forwards and peered.

There was a wide metre-long trail of slime shimmering in the morning sun. It reminded her of the trails that some snails left at the park when she went on walks with her granny. Only very big and not as silvery.

Definitely not as silvery.

This was brown.

She took a step closer.

It was brown, but it sparkled in a way that she hadn't thought it would. That made it slightly better, considering it was slime and brown.

'I wish we had a jar to put some in,' said Arabella. 'Before it's gone. We could scoop it up.'

Mary-Kate shuddered.

'Is there a jar in your backpack?'

'No,' lied Mary-Kate.

'I thought I saw one when your backpack was open at the village green,' said Arabella.

'That has my lucky international coin collection in it,' said Mary-Kate.

'You can put the coins in the front pocket of the backpack,' suggested Arabella.

Mary-Kate took a deep breath. Her lucky things were very important and lucky things shouldn't be tampered with. Lucky things had their own law. You kept them on a shelf and chose them at the right time carefully and it didn't matter if you didn't know how they were lucky they just were, even if they were never touched or used. She didn't know how she was going to explain this to Arabella Woolington.

Then she remembered flashing the lucky novelty torch at Woolington House and how happy she'd been when Arabella had returned her signal. That torch had been very lucky because she'd used it.

Arabella waited patiently while Mary-Kate took out the small jar. She removed the coins one by one and placed them in the backpack's front pocket. There were coins from Ghana, Mauritius and Mozambique. There were coins from Egypt, Mongolia and Uzbekistan. Coins that Professor Martin brought back from every corner of the world.

'I'm not sure I can do the scooping,' said Mary-Kate, handing the jar to Arabella.

'Never mind, I'm good at that.' Arabella raced to a nearby garden, snapped the stem of a large hollyhock and quickly removed the leaves and flowers. 'First you need a slime-scooping stick!'

She knelt down and, using the stick, moved some of the brown sparkling slime into the mouth of the jar. It slid in and down the side of the glass. Mary-Kate looked quickly at the sky.

'Do you think we need more?' asked Arabella.

'No,' said Mary-Kate, not looking. Something was bothering her. Something more than just the slime. There was a small worry, buzzing at the back of her brain, but she couldn't catch it. She felt the stone vibrating beneath her feet and the sound of a car in the distance.

'Quick,' said Arabella, fastening the lid onto the jar. 'It's Papa coming in the rover.'

She handed Mary-Kate the jar, who held it, horrified, until Arabella wrenched it from her hands and placed it in her backpack.

'You really don't like slime, do you?' said Arabella as Lord Woolington drove over the bridge and into the village.

Mary-Kate tried not to think about the slime as she sat with Arabella beneath the oak tree near the green. She tried not to look at it as she took out her notebook and glitter pens. She opened to the updated plan for the day and read out what she'd written to Arabella. Pickles stood nearby finishing off the hedge he'd started eating yesterday.

* Get a photo of the Woolington
  Wyrm

* Meet Arabella and hear her story
* Find out if the WWS got a photo of the wyrm
* Visit Mrs Beattie in the retirement home
* Research worm-like creatures

'Oh, I'm in the plan!' said Arabella excitedly.

Mary-Kate placed a neat tick beside the sentence about the Wyrm Watch Society. She knew they didn't have a photo. The little, niggly, midge-sized worry buzzed again.

'You wrote in my notebook that you'd seen the wyrm,' she started. 'I've been wanting to talk to you about it ever since. I've left these pages blank for what you have to tell me. Why didn't you tell me from the beginning?'

'I'm not meant to talk about it,' said Arabella softly.

'Please tell me, it might help,' said Mary-Kate.

Arabella plucked at some grass by her feet, for once lost for words. Pickles chewed slowly, watching them. Finally, she spoke.

'When I was eight my mother became sick,' she said. Her voice was very quiet. Mary-Kate thought of that secluded part of the graveyard and the towering stone angel. That final name inscribed in the stone.

'My father was away a lot at the hospital and I stayed with my nanny at the house,' continued Arabella. 'I don't really know how to explain it. The world felt upside down, everything was different. I really missed her.'

Arabella chewed on her bottom lip and looked to Mary-Kate to see if she understood. Mary-Kate nodded.

'One night, when the moon was full, I couldn't sleep. I crept out of the room, down the steps and into the conservatory because I wanted to look out at the stables and to check on Pickles. All of a sudden, I had a feeling, a funny feeling in my tummy, like something really exciting was about to happen. I saw the wyrm then. I know you won't believe me.'

Her voice had grown even quieter.

'Of course I believe you,' said Mary-Kate, waiting.

Arabella said nothing for a while, as though summoning up the courage to speak.

'It was a great big long creature sliding fast across the lawn before the maze. It was moving very quickly. *Whoosh*, it slid past, like this,' she blurted out at last and made a motion with her hand. 'Crash! It ran straight into the garden furniture. It knocked over the table and chairs. They were brand-new and they were all smashed to bits.'

Mary-Kate realised she was holding her breath.

'It didn't stop. I could still see it going. It was as long as – as long as a bus, two buses even, and then it disappeared behind Round Hill.'

'Did you tell anyone?'

'I told my nanny. She believed me. I mean, she could see the garden furniture too. Mr Blair had to come and fix it and everything before Papa came home. She wasn't scared though. That's what I remember. She took me by the hand and said I must never, ever mention it. She made me swear. She was my papa's nanny too when he was a child. He was teased at school about being a Woolington, you see. They called him Wyrm. His name is even James. So, he doesn't believe in the wyrm at all. Not one little bit. He wants everything to do with that wyrm to disappear. I thought maybe I could tell him. I mean, I really wanted to tell him when he got home from the hospital, but then ... well, then when he came home, he was so sad ...'

'Your mother?'

Arabella nodded sadly.

'I'm sorry,' said Mary-Kate.

'It's okay,' said Arabella, sitting up straight and smiling. Mary-Kate knew that *okay*. She touched her hand to the pocket containing the lucky silver packet with the seven pieces of gum from her father.

'So, you see, I do believe in the wyrm, because I've seen it,' said Arabella firmly. 'I've crept downstairs lots of other times to watch from the windows in case I saw it again. I've looked at Ms Honey's exhibition when she wasn't paying attention because Woolingtons are never, ever meant to mention the wyrm. So, I'm like an expert in a way. And even if the Wyrm Watch Society didn't get a photo, at least we've got some actual slime in a jar. Could we get it tested by a scientist or something? We could ride Pickles to Lessington to see if there's someone there who will test it.'

The niggling, zipping, pinging worry buzzed very loudly in Mary-Kate's head. She put both her hands over her ears and closed her eyes for five seconds.

'Excuse me, Arabella,' she said at last. 'How did you know that the Wyrm Watch Society didn't get a photo last night?'

Mary-Kate and Arabella ran through the lanes of Woolington Well. Destination: the village library. They needed to warn Ms Honey that there was a spy in their midst.

When Mary-Kate had asked Arabella how she

knew about the events of the evening, she'd looked puzzled.

'I heard Graham tell Papa,' she'd said.

'When?'

'This morning. I was in the stable and I heard them talking out near the Range Rover.'

'What did he say?'

'Papa wanted to know if the Wyrm Watch Society got a photo,' said Arabella. 'Graham said "of course they didn't!" and laughed!'

'Why was Graham there? Didn't he lose his job as driver yesterday?'

Arabella had looked even more puzzled. 'Why would he have lost his job?'

'Because Lord Woolington found out he was a member of the Wyrm Watch Society!' cried Mary-Kate. 'I saw him at the Emergency Meeting.'

'Graham would never be part of the Wyrm Watch Society. He's just like Papa, he doesn't believe in it.'

'He was there last night. It was him with the camera that had no film in it!'

They had both stared at each other, mouths open, before leaping to their feet.

Now, Arabella took all the short cuts she could think of. Behind the bakery, between cottages, through vegetable patches, over fences. They were at the library in a matter of minutes, only to find the door was locked, the CLOSED sign swinging in the morning breeze.

'Where could Ms Honey be?' said Arabella.

'Maybe she went to apply for the stop work order anyway, even without the photos?' suggested Mary-Kate. 'She had all the forms ready and it was on a USB. Maybe she had to go to the next big town, the same place that Terry was taking Moira with her broken arm?'

'Moira had a broken arm?'

'Yes,' said Mary-Kate, trying to slow her breathing. Graham! Grey-haired, perfectly pleasant, dignified Graham! What an actor! He had deliberately arrived with a camera containing no film. He'd been feeding information to Lord Woolington about the Society's next moves. No wonder Lord Woolington had known about the Emergency Meeting. The rumble of heavy machinery interrupted her thoughts. There were the beeping sounds of vehicles reversing and the clang of the construction site fence being moved.

'What on earth is that?' said Mary-Kate. 'It's coming from the construction site.'

Two cement trucks were reversing up the next lane. It was a very tight fit. Mary-Kate watched in horror as one of the huge rotating barrels hit the sign that belonged to a little teashop and toppled it to the ground, crushing it under a wheel.

'This is highly unusual,' Mary-Kate heard her mother say, voice loud and calm. 'I'm afraid I cannot let you proceed. My colleagues have only just arrived from London and a stop work order is still in place.'

Mary-Kate and Arabella could not fit down the lane because of the cement trucks so they ran to the next laneway entrance to see who Professor Martin was talking to. Mary-Kate heard Arabella sigh.

'Oh Papa,' she said sadly.

There was Lord Woolington, papers in hand, looking very cheerful. 'No need to panic,' he was saying. 'I'm merely getting the trucks into position for when your work is done. Every minute costs money in the construction industry.'

Professor Martin still did not look impressed. She had squared her shoulders and raised her chin. Her broad-brimmed hat was tilted back on her head.

'I would like them to stop exactly where they are,' she demanded. 'They are not to enter the site; their movement could cause further collapse of the subterranean passage. There could be further relics in this lower portion of the well.'

Lord Woolington nodded, but Mary-Kate could tell that he was seething as he raised his hands to the reversing machinery.

'A collapsed subterranean tunnel,' said Mary-Kate softly. 'A wyrm. A very cranky wyrm that knocks things over.'

'What are you thinking?' asked Arabella. 'Is your theory arriving?'

'Yes, I think it is. I really need a book about wriggly things,' said Mary-Kate. She didn't like using the word wriggly, of course, yet she had no choice.

'The library is shut. Oh, I wish we knew where Ms Honey was,' said Arabella.

'I think it's okay, I know where another library is,' said Mary-Kate.

They sat on the rug before the small library in the Woolington suite. 'Books on wriggly things. Books on wriggly things,' chanted Arabella, scanning the shelves. 'What kind of wriggly things? Worms? Snakes?'

'I'm not entirely sure,' said Mary-Kate. 'What family do you think the Woolington Wyrm belongs to?'

'Technically I think it's meant to belong to the dragon family?'

Mary-Kate sighed, her eyes moving up and down the spines. There was nothing on dragons. She plucked a book from the shelf. It was an encyclopedia of the natural world.

'This will be good to start,' she said.

Mary-Kate located worms in the index. There were three whole pages on them. Marine worms, flatworms, arrow worms. Roundworms, tapeworms, pinworms. There were plenty of words that made her feel worried: 'helminth' and 'nematode', for instance. And then there was the word 'annelid'. That word gave her a small involuntary shiver.

So did the picture. Mary-Kate looked at the coloured photograph of an annelid. In a way it did remind her very much of a small version of the Woolington Wyrm in the painting.

She read aloud.

'Annelids are segmented worms. If their tail ends are cut off, they can sometimes grow them back again.'

That made her think of the legend, those stories of men with swords cutting the wyrm in half only to have it grow back like new. She continued to read.

'An earthworm is a type of annelid. They can have five or more hearts. They are simultaneously both male and female. They leave behind trails of slime.'

Mary-Kate and Arabella cast a glance at each other.

'Earthworms don't have eyes, but they can sense light. They also feel vibrations.'

Mary-Kate remembered the painting of the wyrm in the village library. She turned to Arabella. 'When you were little and you saw the wyrm, did you notice if it had eyes?'

'I only remember how large and fast it was. Its tail was already moving away before I had time to blink!'

Mary-Kate nodded and kept reading.

'Earthworms can die if exposed to sunlight for too long.

'Earthworms make long tunnels.

'Earthworms sometimes disguise their tunnel with a midden, which is a mound of castings and earth.'

'What is a casting?' said Arabella.

Mary-Kate looked at a diagram opposite those words.

'Poo,' she said, although she didn't want to.

'Yuck,' said Arabella, grinning.

'Tunnels,' said Mary-Kate, softly. She closed her eyes. 'Subterranean tunnels. Sunlight. Slime. Vibrations. Noise. No eyes.'

She opened her notebook and wrote these words down in large raspberry glitter letters. She stared at them for some time.

'Are you okay?' asked Arabella.

'Yes. I think a theory is happening,' said Mary-Kate, solemnly. 'I think it's about tunnels and eyes.'

'That's the theory?' It wasn't that Arabella looked disappointed, more confused. Mary-Kate took a deep breath.

'So, to explain: we have a large wyrm from the dragon family that looks a lot like an oversized earthworm,' she said, turning the picture of the earthworm towards Arabella. 'It doesn't have eyes. I thought they'd forgotten to add them in the painting in the village library. Look how similar this picture is.'

Arabella nodded. She still looked confused.

'And maybe it behaves a bit like an earthworm, too,' said Mary-Kate. 'I mean, number one: it leaves a trail of slime. Number two: it can't see and only feels vibrations. Every time there are lots of changes in the square, it emerges. Maybe it's all the vibrations?'

Arabella said nothing. It made Mary-Kate uncomfortable, but she forged on.

'Maybe it can't see, and it only knows its way around by touch? After all, it has lived here for centuries. And when something changes, well, that's when things go wrong. Remember Mr Blair said the wall was new? Bang, the wyrm crashed straight into it. Remember you said the garden furniture on your back lawn was new? The wyrm smashed right through it.'

Arabella still hadn't said anything. It made Mary-Kate even more worried. She took a deep breath and continued.

'Also, maybe since the well was damaged,

too much light is entering where it lives, and it doesn't like that.'

Mary-Kate felt her theory was getting wobblier by the minute.

'Which brings me to tunnels. Some stories say that the wyrm lives in the well. Some say it lives in Round Hill. What if it lives in-between? What if a tunnel goes between those places? What if the wyrm goes in at Round Hill and out at the well? Only now it can't, and everything is messed up and it's angry!'

Arabella was staring at her, her mouth slightly open.

Mary-Kate felt that familiar sinking sensation. The one when she said the wrong thing during small talk. The one where Amelia Blythe-Tompkinson looked at her just the same way. Her cheeks began to smart.

'It's a silly theory, isn't it?' she said.

Arabella shook her head.

'It's absolutely brilliant!' she cried.

Monster hunter Professor Lavinia Lightfoot famously once said, 'People who have seen a monster are usually a lot more interesting than people who haven't.'

P.K. Mayberry's Complete Guide to Monsters of the Northern Hemisphere

Certain things made Mary-Kate feel good. Dresses with pockets, for instance, neatly sliced watermelon and blue-lined notepads. And, she decided, being able to tick things off her list in her quest to solve the mystery of a large fire-breathing wyrm.

* Talk to Arabella and hear her story ✓
* Research worm-like creatures ✓

'That just leaves visiting Mrs Beattie and getting a photo of the wyrm,' said Mary-Kate. 'Do you think they'll let us talk to her at the retirement home?'

'That's where my nanny is,' said Arabella. 'I'm always visiting her, so they know me there.'

The retirement home was beyond the village square, so they decided to stop by the library first to check if Yolanda had returned. They were glad to find the door to the library unlocked and the librarian dragging a box from a back room.

'Oh, hello,' she said absent-mindedly, lifting a chain and padlock from the box. 'You haven't seen Graham, have you? He was meant to come by and help with this.'

Mary-Kate and Arabella cast glances at each other.

'What is it that you're doing?' asked Mary-Kate, tentatively.

'I'm preparing to padlock myself to a post in the square in the case that the new stop work order fails. Professor Martin's colleagues are meeting as we speak. The rumours from the construction site are that they don't think there is anything of great significance at the bottom of the well. So, if that's the case this is what I'll have to do. If I chain myself then the foundations can't be poured. I don't mind you hearing this, Lady Arabella, because I know you to care about the wyrm, deep down. You must.

I've seen you in here countless times since you were small, looking at the Wyrm Exhibit.'

Arabella blushed crimson.

'I do care,' she whispered. 'Only, we've something to tell you.'

'Good or bad?' said Yolanda, searching their faces.

'Both,' said Mary-Kate.

The librarian sat down, the large padlock still in her hands.

'The good news is that we have a theory,' said Mary-Kate. 'Well, a kind of theory. It's a bit messy. We think the wyrm is like a very large segmented annelid.'

'From the dragon family,' chimed in Arabella.

'And it's made a big tunnel between Round Hill and the well. Whenever there's a lot of noise or vibrations in the square it becomes angry. And since the well was damaged, too much light is getting into the tunnel down there. It doesn't have eyes, but it can sense light. Its tunnel has collapsed a lot too, so it can't come and go the way it likes to, and it has to turn around down below the village.'

'And that's what causes the earth tremors,' added Arabella.

'It's only since the well was broken up last Saturday that the wyrm has reappeared,' finished Mary-Kate.

Yolanda listened to them politely.

'Well done, girls,' she said kindly. 'However, I'm sorry to say none of this is going to help us with proof of the wyrm. The cement trucks have arrived. Professor Martin and her colleagues from London are down in the well and if they decide they've recovered all they need then … Theories won't really help, I'm afraid. I do wish Graham would hurry up.'

'That's the other thing we wanted to tell you,' said Arabella, slowly.

Arabella took the padlock from Yolanda's hands and Mary-Kate replaced it with a cup of tea. They comforted her. *Arabella is best at it*, Mary-

Kate thought. She, herself, was unsure of what to say when someone turned out to be dastardly and devious rather than honest and dignified.

'He's been such a good member, for almost a year now,' said Yolanda.

'Have some tea,' said Arabella, patting her. 'We're very sorry to tell you this.'

'Oh girls,' sighed the librarian. 'Tell me what you plan to do next?'

'We're going to see Mrs Beattie at the retirement home,' said Mary-Kate. 'We're hoping she can help us in some way.'

'Perhaps you're right,' said Yolanda, sighing deeply again. 'She'll be very disappointed in all of us from the society. Look at us: Moira has a broken arm, Terry keeps hiding under things and Graham wasn't even one of us.'

She began to cry quite loudly then, and it made tears spring into Mary-Kate's eyes. She couldn't bear to see anyone crying.

'Please don't give up yet,' said Arabella. 'Mary-

Kate and I will come back as soon as we can.'

'We're going to solve this,' promised Mary-Kate.

They went via the square, peering through the tall metal fencing. The cement trucks were rumbling in the side streets, waiting. There was the Professor and her colleagues as well, standing together at the edge of the far side of the square, their heads bowed over a large piece of paper. *Best not to bother her*, thought Mary-Kate, although she had so much to tell her.

Professor Martin looked up suddenly, as though sensing that Mary-Kate was nearby, the way she always did.

'Everything okay?' she called.

Mary-Kate raised her thumb.

Everything wasn't okay, but there was still time to *make* it okay. Right then, she truly believed it. She had a strawberry-scented notebook full of evidence;

a slippery, wobbly theory; a jar containing wyrm slime and a new friend in Lady Arabella Woolington. Anything seemed possible.

'Take the umbrella, Mary-Kate,' shouted Professor Martin. 'I've left it near the fence there. I think it might rain.'

Mrs Beattie was seated near her window in a wheelchair, watching the downpour. She wore a serene expression on her face. She also wore a blue and white polka dot dressing-gown, and her hair was like pink fairy floss on her head. She turned when they entered.

'Some young ones to see you,' said the matron, who had allowed them in. 'Lady Arabella Woolington herself and her friend Mary-Kate. What did you say your last name was?'

'Martin,' said Mary-Kate.

'Mary-Kate Martin, the Professor's daughter?' said Mrs Beattie, excitedly. 'I was so hoping you'd come. And hello Arabella, I'm glad you're here too, of course.'

Mary-Kate remembered Yolanda saying it was Mrs Beattie who encouraged the Wyrm Watch Society to contact the Prof.

'Do you know my mother?' asked Mary-Kate, stepping forwards.

'Yes, I've met her a few times over the years,' said Mrs Beattie, motioning to a large chair before the window. 'Come, come, sit down.'

Arabella and Mary-Kate sat in the armchair side by side.

'Look at you both.' Mrs Beattie grinned. 'Just the sight I needed to see today! You are here about the wyrm, no doubt.'

'Did you know it's come back?' said Arabella. 'Twice since Sunday.'

'Oh yes, so I've heard,' said Mrs Beattie, a wistful look on her face. 'I wanted to climb out of my window last night and go running to look for it like I did when I was a girl. You've seen it, haven't you Arabella?'

Arabella gasped, turned pink again. 'How do you know?'

'I can read it on someone's face,' said Mrs Beattie. 'Many people have seen it and they almost all look a certain way when they mention it.'

'Many people?' repeated Mary-Kate.

'Why, yes. I've met many over the years. Not many of them ever wanted to be named, though. That's the way it is when one sees such mysterious and magnificent monsters. People don't know what to do. What will people think if they say they've seen it? Some might tell their closest friends. Some others tell no one and keep it a secret forever.'

She looked at Arabella kindly.

'What happened the day you saw it?' Mary-Kate took her notebook out as she spoke and prepared a pink glitter pen to match Mrs Beattie's hair.

'It was an awfully long time ago, Mary-Kate, though I remember it like it was yesterday,' began Mrs Beattie. 'I was near Round Hill. I went there often with my dogs. There are all sorts of little rocks and crags but only one cave called Wyrm Hole. Have you heard of it?'

'Yes,' said Arabella and Mary-Kate in unison.

'I went there because it was normally peaceful. That day, there was a lot of noise. They had dug up the town square, you know, to lay new pipes that year and there was so much banging and clanking in town that it reached all the way across the fields. I was standing with the dogs, quite near Round Hill, when there was a terrific crash from in town. I heard later that a large pipe had been dropped by a crane, narrowly missing some men. It was an enormous bang, and then ... well, then it happened.'

Mary-Kate and Arabella leaned forwards.

'First the dogs started barking at the entrance to Wyrm Hole and then the earth started trembling beneath my feet. I called the dogs, but they wouldn't come away from the hole, so I ran to fetch them. I had a feeling something terribly exciting was about to happen. Even *before* it happened. Have you ever had that feeling?'

Arabella nodded solemnly.

'The hairs stood up on my arms. I was pulling the dogs back and trying to peer into the hole when it came out. Oh, it came out with such a rush. It came right at me roaring, and its breath was so bad, and it gave me such a fright that I nearly died there and then.'

Mary-Kate was hunched, holding her breath, hanging on to every one of Mrs Beattie's words. Arabella had her hands over her heart.

'I ducked, you see, or it might have accidentally

roasted me. And then I scrambled up onto my feet and started running down the hill, the dogs in front of me. When I looked back, I could see its monstrous body and its skin gleaming in the sun. It was coming right for me. I don't think I've ever run so fast in my life! After I'd got halfway down the side of the hill I turned, just in time to see its tail disappearing down into Wyrm Hole again.'

'What happened then?' whispered Mary-Kate.

'I ran home of course, and half the village went back up the hill to see what they could see. They went into the cave and the passage that winds away from it. They said it went no further than it ever did. They suggested I had been imagining things. I knew I hadn't. I saw the wyrm all right. And to this day I consider myself lucky that I did.'

'Even though you were scared?' said Mary-Kate.

'Yes, even though I was ever so scared.' Mrs Beattie smiled again, remembering. 'And do you know what? Something always made me wonder if the wyrm was afraid too.'

'I hadn't thought of it being scared,' said Mary-Kate, thoughtfully. 'Our theory is it doesn't like all the vibrations. We think it can't see and only senses. It only ever causes trouble when there is something happening in the square and there's lots of noise. We also think there's a tunnel between Round Hill and the well, that maybe now the well is damaged too much light is being let in. We don't think it likes light. We think it needs help.'

'Yes. That's why I'm so glad you're here, Mary-Kate,' said Mrs Beattie. 'The Woolington Wyrm definitely needs help.'

'But how do we help it?' asked Mary-Kate. All the research and evidence wasn't going to help if the foundations were poured. There would be so much noise if a big shopping centre was built on top of where the wyrm lived. If many more cars drove in and out of the village each day. If trucks came and went delivering goods. If trees were chopped down and car parks were built.

'You girls have done well so far; research and

theories are very important. There's something else, however, that monster hunters do.'

'Monster hunters?' whispered Mary-Kate.

'By "monster hunters" I mean the good type. There are those that hunt monsters to harm them and there are those that hunt monsters to *help* them. You, Mary-Kate, with your wonderful assistant Arabella, are most definitely the latter.'

'Monster hunters,' said Mary-Kate again, softly, pondering the strange set of words. Was she really a monster hunter? 'What do they do?'

'I think I already know,' said Arabella, putting up her arm like she was in class.

'Yes, Arabella?'

'They go in search of the monster.'

'Well done, Arabella,' said Mrs Beattie, clapping her hands. 'You are correct. I've been searching for the Woolington Wyrm ever since I saw it that day as a child. I've slept beside the Wyrm Hole. I've organised explorations and founded the Wyrm Watch Society. The wyrm is a secretive and quiet thing, I've come to realise, doing no one any harm. And now it's in trouble and you are our only hope. Open the drawer over there please, Arabella, I have something I would like to give you and Mary-Kate. Pull out the long blue box.'

Arabella did as she was told and returned with an old, thin velvet box.

'Open it,' said Mrs Beattie.

Arabella, seated in the chair beside Mary-Kate again, opened the box. Inside there was a medal on a tricoloured ribbon. The ribbon was magenta, blue and green.

The bronze medal was star-shaped and in the middle there were words written in another language.

'What does it say?' said Arabella.

'Is that Latin?' asked Mary-Kate.

'Perhaps a little homework for you, Mary-Kate,' said Mrs Beattie. 'This medal was given to me a long time ago. I'm hoping that it will bring you both luck when you go to Round Hill to help the Woolington Wyrm.'

It is most likely that in any monster hunter's adventure there will come a time that they must make a decision: to enter the lair or not?

P.K. Mayberry's Complete Guide to Monsters of the Northern Hemisphere

Arabella sat astride Pickles, the medal pinned to her chest. The girls had both decided she could wear it first. If it was to bring them luck, they'd have to take turns. They'd both also agreed that Pickles would be the fastest way to get to Round Hill. Pickles was not in favour of this plan.

'Come on, Pickles,' said Arabella, trying to get him to lift his head from the grass he was eating.

The rain had stopped but the sky was grey and miserable. Mary-Kate sat behind Arabella, her arms clasped around her waist. She wore Arabella's helmet and she had slid her mother's large black umbrella down into the space between her back and her backpack, hooking the curved end over one of the straps. It made her feel almost entirely not like a monster hunter.

A monster hunter would have a reliable form of transport and they probably wouldn't carry an umbrella. They'd wear a special monster-hunting suit.

'Maybe it would be quicker to run?' she suggested as Pickles continued to chew thoughtfully on the grass.

'No, he'll get the hang of it in a minute,' said Arabella. 'He usually does.'

'The hang of walking?' asked Mary-Kate. *No wonder he came last in showjumping.*

Eventually, Arabella manoeuvred Pickles away from the long grass and he began to move, stopping every so often to see if there were other bits of grass that he might like to taste. Arabella was right, though. He did get the hang of it and after about five minutes he started to trot in a slow manner. He whinnied once as if he was almost enjoying himself.

'Good boy,' said Arabella.

They trotted through the fields, Arabella knowing just which gates to take. Lonely, grey Woolington House loomed large and behind it, Round Hill.

Finally, Arabella helped Mary-Kate down and led Pickles by the reins around the hill's base. A wind blew on the hill, rolling the grass in waves, and it was very quiet apart from that sound. She tethered Pickles to a fence.

'Wyrm Hole is up there,' said Arabella.

The hill was studded with boulders, some much taller than them, leaning at strange angles or against each other, creating dark tunnels and rock archways. They picked their way past these giant stones beneath a sky that had grown dark with storm clouds. They were almost at the summit of the hill when they heard the growl of an engine.

'Who is it?' whispered Mary-Kate as they dropped down behind some rocks. Arabella, finger on lips, darted forwards to the cover of another large rock and peered down over the side.

'Two men,' she whispered, her eyes widening. 'And a bulldozer.'

Mary-Kate crept next to Arabella and peered over the rock. There was a man stepping from a small truck and another jumping down from a large yellow bulldozer.

'Wyrm Hole is up high, around the back there,'

said the first man. 'Do you think you can get the bulldozer that way? We want one of those big boulders moved over the entrance.'

The other man looked worried.

'I can't get the bulldozer up that high. We probably need a small bobcat to work on that steep incline. The only problem is that a small bobcat won't lift a big rock like that.'

'Well, what will?' asked the first man.

'A crane?' suggested the other, scratching his head.

'And where do we get a crane from?' demanded the first, exasperated.

'Well, I'll have to drive to Lessington, won't I,' said the bulldozer driver. 'And that'll be about half an hour. Then back again. And I haven't had my afternoon tea yet.'

'Afternoon tea?' shouted the first man. 'The boss wants this plugged *now*.' He sighed. 'Okay, go to Lessington and get the crane. Be back here in an hour. That'll have to do.'

Mary-Kate and Arabella stayed crouched for some time, even after the sound of the engine had faded. The dark clouds scudded across the sky. Arabella plucked at the grass, thinking.

'We have to stop this from happening,' she said, at last. 'I wish I knew how.'

'I know how,' said Mary-Kate. 'We need a photograph of the wyrm. And we've only got an hour.'

Wyrm Hole was a small round cave and Mary-Kate felt worried even looking at it. She remembered what Yolanda had said. Wyrm Hole had been investigated. The tunnel did not extend far into the hill. What could she possibly hope to find?

'Should I go alone?' said Mary-Kate. 'And you stay here to stop the bulldozer?'

Arabella's eyes widened.

'I'm definitely coming with you,' she said. 'Can't we leave a note? A page from your notebook. That'll stop them moving a boulder over the entrance.'

Mary-Kate wrote the note in large raspberry glitter block letters.

WE ARE INSIDE THE TUNNEL! DO NOT BLOCK OFF!!

They placed it at the cave entrance and the wind snatched it quickly, somersaulting it in the air.

Arabella caught it just in time.

'How are we going to secure it?' Mary-Kate sighed.

'I have an idea,' said Arabella. She folded the piece of paper and raced down the hill towards where Pickles was tied. She placed the piece of paper underneath his bridle. She untethered him. Mary-Kate watched from above as Arabella spoke to her pony, waving her arms and pointing to town. Pickles seemed very bored by these instructions and bent his head down again to eat grass.

'I told him to race to town if we weren't back out before they came back with the crane,' said Arabella as she made it back to the top of the hill.

Mary-Kate nodded politely.

'That's great,' she said. 'In case he doesn't want to though, I'm going to leave another note here.'

She wrote a new note hastily and then closed her eyes, touching the pocket of her navy dress gently. She had never contemplated doing dangerous things. Not once. Little things made her worried. Small talk. Brown pencils. Sitting backwards on trains.

Yet here she was at the entrance to a cave where a large fire-breathing wyrm lived, she was sure of it. And this large fire-breathing wyrm needed help.

Strangely, in a way that made her feel quite calm, Mary-Kate knew she was the person who would be good at helping it.

She took the lucky silver packet containing the seven last pieces of gum that her father left behind. She squeezed a piece out and popped it in her mouth.

It was no longer fresh and she tried not to worry about that.

It was sticky and that's what mattered.

Arabella watched her.

'Sorry I can't offer you any,' said Mary-Kate as she chewed. 'It's my lucky gum. It belonged to my father before he went missing. I was only five.'

'Your father went missing?' gasped Arabella.

'On Mount Shishapangma,' said Mary-Kate. She didn't think she'd ever said that out loud before. 'It's in Tibet.'

'Sorry,' said Arabella.

'It's okay,' said Mary-Kate, straightening her shoulders and smiling. She took the gum from her mouth and stuck the note to the cave entrance. 'Are you sure you want to come?'

'Absolutely,' said Arabella Woolington.

Most monster hunters complete a safety
checklist before dangerous missions.
Professor Lavinia Lightfoot always kept
hers in a distinctive yellow handbag.

P.K. Mayberry's Complete Guide to
Monsters of the Northern Hemisphere

Mary-Kate used her mobile phone torch and Arabella held the novelty Big Ben torch and the passage was illuminated. Mary-Kate's red sparkly shoes were lit up too, and that was comforting.

'It smells a bit in here,' said Arabella.

A musty, dank smell. Mary-Kate wrinkled her nose. They moved along the passage, hunching their shoulders as they went, and when the tunnel grew narrower, Arabella suggested they move on their hands and knees.

That seemed like a bad idea to Mary-Kate, because the ground was dirty. It was a cave, after all. Arabella, who always had dirty knees, took the lead with gusto.

'Like this,' she called back. 'It's much easier.'

She had put the Big Ben torch in her mouth to keep a light ahead of them. Mary-Kate placed her hands on the ground. It was damp. Damp and cool in a way that made her shudder. *But not slimy*, she reminded herself. And that was a positive. Mary-Kate and Arabella crawled in silence for a long time, mainly because Arabella had the torch in her mouth. Mary-Kate was sure she'd be talking if that wasn't the case.

She wished Arabella was talking. She'd decided Arabella talking nonstop was calming, especially when in a dank, dark cave.

Now the tunnel was very dark, their small beams of light seemed puny and this was beginning to seem like a bad idea. A very big, bad idea. She glanced back and saw that the entrance to Wyrm Hole had disappeared, the sunlight with it, and the idea seemed *hugely* bad. As bad as an avalanche on the side of a mountain. Thunderously, catastrophically bad. She began to breathe fast, small little gasps of air. And then Arabella stopped abruptly in front of her.

'Oh, it's ended,' Arabella said in dismay, sitting on

her bottom and shining the lucky Big Ben torch at the wall ahead. 'A dead end. They always say that's what's down here. How could that be? How can the wyrm get through?'

'Oh well,' gasped Mary-Kate, with the tiny amount of air she had in her lungs. 'I guess we should head back.'

She felt a tiny bit relieved that they wouldn't have to go any further and this allowed a slightly larger portion of air into her lungs.

'Are you all right?' asked Arabella, shining the torch full in Mary-Kate's face. 'You sound funny.'

Mary-Kate squinted against the light.

'Ouch,' she said.

'Sorry,' said Arabella. 'There must be a way through.'

She was on her hands and knees, crawling up and down in front of the dead end, torch back in her mouth.

'It's really soft here,' she said, 'and it's a bit raised, a kind of mound.'

She shone the torch on a patch of the dank cave floor.

'Really soft and squidgy,' she repeated. 'Come and feel?'

Mary-Kate definitely did *not* want to touch dank mud that was soft and squidgy. She was only just getting her air back, yet she moved forwards to the place that Arabella was enthusiastically patting.

'Can I borrow the umbrella, please? I'm sure it's completely different to the other floor,' Arabella said as Mary-Kate sat beside her. She took the umbrella from where she'd hooked it into her backpack.

Arabella grabbed it by the handle, inverted the umbrella and began banging the muddy mound with the pointy tip.

'Oh, look,' she said. 'It sinks right in.'

'Maybe stop—' started Mary-Kate, but it was too late.

The mound of soft squidgy dirt had disappeared.

So had the cave floor.

And both of them were falling.

They slid down very quickly; there was no stopping it. It was as though a trapdoor had opened and they were on a muddy, slippery slide. Arabella yelled very loudly as they slid.

'We're sliiiiiiiiiiiidiiiiiiiiing!' she yelled.

Mary-Kate slid in a quieter fashion.

Where are we going? she thought. *How are we going to get back out?*

That made her worried, so she stopped thinking that.

'La-la-la,' she tried as she slid. Then, when that didn't work, she tried some critical thinking.

The wyrm must make a sort of trapdoor, she started, *out of dirt and mud and slime and poo, so no one can find its lair. A midden!*

Slime.

'La-la-la,' she said again, louder.

'We're still sliiiiiiiiiiiidiiiiiiiing!' yelled Arabella,

keeping Mary-Kate updated.

Lair? thought Mary-Kate, pondering that word. Were they sliding directly into the Woolington Wyrm's lair?

This thought seemed even worse than slime and poo, so she was grateful that her bottom hit the floor with such a thud that she was winded and didn't have to think that thought anymore.

'Ouch,' said Arabella.

They had landed in a much larger tunnel. They stood up gingerly and both looked back the way they'd come, shining their weak torches at what was indeed a very large, earthen slippery dip. They were deep inside Round Hill. The torch light illuminated the tendrils of roots sticking out from the slide and Mary-Kate wondered if they could use them to climb back up when they needed to. *That* definitely seemed like something a monster hunter would do. Arabella handed her back the black umbrella that had caused all the trouble.

'Thank you,' said Mary-Kate. 'I guess we'd better

keep going.' She tried to sound brave and Arabella agreed in a small squeaky voice. Her small squeaky voice echoed in the tunnel and Mary-Kate knew she was scared.

'Everything will be all right,' reassured Mary-Kate.

'Keep going' was a plan of sorts and that's what they needed right now, Mary-Kate decided. Plans were good, even if they were as simple as that. Keep going. One red sparkly footstep in front of the other.

The light from their tiny torches showed the walls of the tunnel ahead began to curve. Arabella was still very quiet.

'If we ever do this again, I think we should be more organised,' Mary-Kate said, to make conversation. 'A larger torch, for instance. I think a proper monster hunter would have a larger torch.'

'Definitely a larger torch,' agreed Arabella.

'Maybe some rope with a hook on the end to climb back up that slope,' said Mary-Kate. Arabella made a small scared noise, as though she didn't like thinking about how they were going to get back up.

'And a dog,' added Mary-Kate, quickly. 'It could stay at the hole to bark and let people know that we're down here.'

That had to be better than a strawberry-scented notebook page attached to a rock with chewing gum.

'Could the dog be small and yellow and have a name like Popcorn?' asked Arabella softly.

'Yes,' said Mary-Kate.

This conversation seemed to help them both feel better as they walked. They decided Popcorn would wear a sparkly blue collar with a silver bell. He would be very clever and know how to do all sorts of tricks like jumping through hoops. He'd probably have a second name too. It would be either Snowball or Curly.

'We've been going forever,' said Arabella, after some time. 'I bet we're way across the fields. I bet we're almost underneath the village.'

Every one of their words was repeated softly by the walls.

'I've lost track of how long we've been walking,' said Mary-Kate and then she remembered her phone. She checked the time. 'It's only been twenty minutes.'

There was a dripping sound in the dark tunnel. Mary-Kate held her phone torch high and the dripping walls loomed large.

One sparkly red footstep in front of another.

'If we meet the Woolington Wyrm, what should we do?' she asked. She realised this was probably something they should have thought of earlier.

'We should say, "hello, sorry to bother you. We really need a photo to prove your existence so that we can save you".'

They both giggled, very nervous giggles, in the tunnel.

'Maybe it will be asleep?' said Mary-Kate, hopefully. 'I'll take the photo and then say "Run!"'

'Yes, it will probably be asleep,' said Arabella. 'It'll be snoring.'

More nervous giggles and then Arabella stopped still.

'What was that?' she said.

'What?' squeaked Mary-Kate.

'I heard a sound,' said Arabella.

'What kind of sound?'

She'd already heard it though. She froze and then found she couldn't unfreeze. Her sparkly red shoes were stuck to the ground.

It was a scraping noise coming from up ahead.

A scraping, scratching noise, coming from somewhere behind.

A scraping, scratching, clanging noise coming from somewhere she wasn't quite sure.

And it was getting louder.

Mary-Kate didn't feel that something exciting was about to happen, the way Arabella had. Or the way Mrs Beattie had. That was disappointing. She only felt completely terrified.

The sound was coming from everywhere. Arabella ran into Mary-Kate because she thought the sound was coming from ahead. Mary-Kate ran into Arabella because she thought the sound was from behind. She'd never had an instinct that a large fire-breathing wyrm was somewhere nearby, but her legs seemed to want to run forwards and she decided to trust them. They seemed the most sensible part of her.

'This way,' she squeaked forcefully. She turned Arabella and they began to run.

Their torchlights flickered wildly on the walls, and the tunnel was loud with scraping and scratching. It swirled in the air around them and it was definitely in front of them now, Mary-Kate decided, which was terrible because her legs didn't seem to be able to stop running that way; they had a life of their own. She was concentrating so hard on slowing them down that she didn't realise at first that she wasn't running anymore, rather that she was flying. Her feet had left the floor because the floor had suddenly given way again. She was flying with Arabella through the air for several seconds before the ground rushed up to hit her in the knees, followed by her elbows and then her chin.

'Ouch!' said Arabella for the second time that day.

'Quickly, while the Professor is gone,' said a voice quite near.

'Pardon?' whispered Mary-Kate, the air knocked out of her.

It seemed a very strange thing to say to someone who had just had a nasty fall. Her knees were bleeding, she was quite sure of it. She could feel a sticky substance on her stockings. The ground moved ever so slightly beneath her hands and knees in a worrying way.

'I need you to help me attach this pipe to those cylinders,' said the same voice, which sounded familiar. There was more scraping and scratching, then metal on metal. 'Yes, that pipe there.'

Mary-Kate saw Arabella's eyes widen and her

mouth open – she was going to shout. It was Lord Woolington.

'No, wait,' whispered Mary-Kate.

They must have made it all the way to beneath the village square, close to the partially collapsed subterranean tunnel that led to the old well. There was faint light entering the small circular cavern they knelt in. Lord Woolington must be somewhere above them. Mary-Kate flicked open her phone to check for service. There was none. She opened a voice memo app instead and hit the record button. She motioned for Arabella to lower the Big Ben torch.

'We'll need all three canisters,' said Lord Woolington.

'What is this stuff, Sir?' another voice asked. 'I'm not sure about this anymore.'

Graham? mouthed Mary-Kate.

Arabella nodded.

'What do you mean you're not sure about it?' said Lord Woolington. 'We know this is where it lives. Somewhere between here and Round Hill. It's made the lives of the Woolingtons misery for seven centuries. And today I'm going to get rid of it once and for all. You promised you'd help me in exchange for the manager's job at the shopping centre. Please tell me you've got the rock over the other end at Round Hill?'

Mary-Kate placed a hand on Arabella's arm. Lord Woolington knew the wyrm was real!

'It's happening as we speak,' replied Graham.

'Good. See that generator, that's going to power this pump,' said Lord Woolington. 'This gas will put it to sleep. The company I've engaged will deal with the rest. Who would have thought there were actual people who capture these creatures! If I'd known I would have done it sooner. No longer will Woolington Well be known as the home of a very large worm or the Woolington name be tarnished by its legend.'

'How will they deal with it?' stammered Graham. 'I mean, it might be asleep, but it's still trapped down there. How will they get it out?'

'That's their problem,' replied Lord Woolington. 'They said they're quite used to these relocation issues.'

'I'm not sure I can,' said Graham. 'I'm sorry. I've been thinking about it all morning. I've seen it now. Or part of it—'

'Go and get some lunch, Graham,' interrupted Lord Woolington. 'Pretend you never saw me here. I've got to do what's right for the village of Woolington Well and the Woolington name.'

There was silence. A long silence. Mary-Kate waited, her heart bang-bang-banging in her ears. The ground quivered beneath her.

'Please don't go. Please don't go. Please don't go,' whispered Arabella.

'I'll just go and grab a bite to ...' started Graham but his words were swallowed up by another sound.

A loud hissing sound.

The sleeping gas was being pumped into the tunnel.

A monster hunter will learn quickly
that there is nearly always a time to run.

P.K. Mayberry's Complete Guide to
Monsters of the Northern Hemisphere

'**P**apa!' shouted Arabella over the sudden roar of a generator. 'Stop!'

'We have to get out of here, Arabella!' cried Mary-Kate. She stood up and slipped immediately on the sticky stuff that was not just on her knees but beneath her feet too. 'Quickly!'

Mary-Kate shone the torch up to the ledge they'd fallen from. It wasn't too high. They could easily pull themselves up if they helped each other.

'Hold my hand,' she said to Arabella, who was still shouting frantically to her father. 'He can't hear you. We'll have to get out the other way.'

The hissing sound was even louder. The generator was roaring. Mary-Kate noticed the earth was trembling. She felt a strange feeling in the pit of her belly, a feeling that something exciting was about to happen.

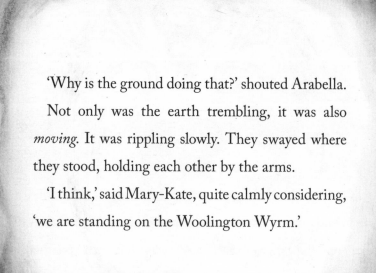

'Why is the ground doing that?' shouted Arabella.

Not only was the earth trembling, it was also *moving*. It was rippling slowly. They swayed where they stood, holding each other by the arms.

'I think,' said Mary-Kate, quite calmly considering, 'we are standing on the Woolington Wyrm.'

Arabella and Mary-Kate turned their torches to the ground. There was lots of slime. Lots of brown slime. Lots of brown slime attached to the Woolington Wyrm and the Woolington Wyrm was coiled in the small cavern looking very cranky. They knew it was cranky because it had lifted its head. It certainly didn't look pleased.

It looked even more fearsome than it had in the painting in the village library. Its head rose up from the middle of its slimy coils. It had two rather crooked horns above a bulbous nose, beneath which glistened a mixed assortment of jagged teeth. The teeth glinted by the light of their small torches. The Woolington Wyrm had no eyes, although there was a deep red area that glowed above its nose.

'Hello,' whispered Mary-Kate. She thought it was probably best to try to sound friendly. Arabella stared, speechless, at the wyrm.

Mary-Kate wondered if the wyrm knew friendly. Perhaps it only knew screaming and yelling and people with swords.

'I'm not here to hurt you,' she whispered. Which immediately seemed silly. After all, even its head was twice as large as her. Also, the generator was still roaring, so it probably couldn't hear her. And what if her theory was correct and it couldn't hear at all, it could only feel vibrations?

'I'd actually like to help you,' she continued, just in case it could hear. 'I see what's happening. Your well has been damaged and there's light coming in and there's been so much noise. It was the same all those years ago when Mrs Beattie saw you and they were laying the pipes. And then one hundred years before with the new inn and so on. You don't like noise at all. You like peace and quiet.'

She was talking a lot. She knew it.

'We want to help you. What we need is a photo. If we have proof of you then the shopping centre will be stopped. And everything will go back to the way it was.'

The wyrm turned its head slightly towards her.

She thought she was doing quite well. She felt

more positive now that she'd got all that out. Then the Woolington Wyrm opened its mouth and Mary-Kate saw the rest of its sharp teeth. The ones inside its mouth were much neater than those on the outside. There were several sets inside, lined up one behind each other. The Woolington Wyrm gave Mary-Kate a nice, long look at them. Arabella clutched her arm and whimpered.

When the wyrm was done showing what it had inside its mouth, it made a vile hissing noise, accompanied by a bad smell: part slime, part filthy teeth …

Perhaps the wyrm was trying to communicate with her, only she didn't know what it was saying?

Maybe it was saying, *Here are my teeth. I'd like to eat you with them.*

Or maybe it was saying, *You are absolutely correct. Your theory is spot on.*

It breathed some fire then and Mary-Kate decided, as she ducked out of the way, pulling Arabella down with her, that it probably wasn't the latter.

'That's not very polite,' said Mary-Kate, crouched on the ground that was really the Woolington Wyrm.

It made a noise in reply. It wasn't a very happy noise.

'Please let me speak,' said Mary-Kate, although she didn't stand up in case it blasted her with fire again. 'The thing is ... If the shopping centre is built, there will never be peace here again. We need to stop that.'

'Quick, take a photo,' said Arabella.

But it was too late. Mary-Kate wrenched Arabella to the side as the wyrm blasted fire and the flame licked up to the cavern ceiling. The fire seemed to suck up a lot of oxygen in the cavern and Mary-Kate felt her lungs ache.

'Okay,' she wheezed, 'so I'm thinking you don't understand me ...'

The wyrm bowed its head and made a low gurgling noise, the place above its nose glowed a deep red. Mary-Kate figured it was brewing up more fire. Its head was coming closer.

In the seconds before the wyrm let forth more

flame, Mary-Kate yelled to Arabella: 'Hold on to me!'

In one movement, she swung the hook of the umbrella up and latched onto one of the wyrm's horns. She dragged herself up, Arabella clutching her waist, and clambered onto the wyrm's head as another fireball erupted. They clung to the long, greasy tufts of hair-like fibres that covered the wyrm's back, breathing hard.

The wyrm threw its head back, enraged.

'No, wait!' cried Mary-Kate, grabbing onto the greasy strands and pulling herself further along the wyrm's back. 'I promise we're trying to help you!'

The wyrm jerked forwards and they nearly lost their balance. It was moving upwards and towards the ledge they'd fallen from. It was writhing in the space, trying to get its huge body to follow. The walls shook and dirt rained from the walls.

Mary-Kate reached for Arabella's hand and they leaped off the wyrm's back, onto the ledge they'd fallen from. They scrambled, bringing their feet up just in time before another ball of fire was released. There was the smell of slightly singed sparkly red shoes.

'Move!' said Arabella. It was her turn now to drag Mary-Kate to her feet.

The walls were shaking as the wyrm's giant body turned in the small cavern. There was terrible angry hissing. It grew louder and louder in Mary-Kate's ears.

HHHHIIIIIISSSSSS!

HHHHIIIIIIISSSSSS!

HHHHIIIIIIISSSSSS!

There was a new taste on the tip of Mary-Kate's tongue. A sour taste that made her cough, followed by a terrible smell clogging her nostrils and making it difficult to breathe.

'The gas,' gasped Arabella. 'Papa! No!'

Mary-Kate quickly swung her backpack off her shoulder and unzipped it. She thrust her hand down inside. Notebook, glitter pens, jar containing slime. Her first- and second-favourite lucky oversized handkerchiefs.

'Here, tie this over your mouth and nose,' she cried to Arabella, passing her one as they ran.

They were at the slope then, clutching at the tendrils of roots, pulling themselves up. Mary-Kate hoped that the note was still there on the rock, that the crane driver had seen it … or even that Pickles had made it to town … *Pickles.*

For some reason, the thought of Pickles doing such a thing made Mary-Kate giggle. And as she giggled, she yawned.

'Run,' she said and then yawned again. Her arms

were weak. Beside her, Arabella let go of the root she was holding and slid back down the way they'd come.

GAS, Mary-Kate thought as she let go and slid down too. She lay beside Arabella on the ground and took her hand. Arabella's eyes were closed. She saw the medal Mrs Beattie had given them glinting on Arabella's chest. It hadn't helped them. They weren't safe. They weren't lucky.

GGGGGAAAAASSSSSSSSSSSSS, she thought, and the word stretched out slowly in her head. Gas and fireballs didn't mix.

Her eyelids drooped. She could see redness in the distance, the glowing red of the wyrm's head. It was coming closer.

'Stop,' she said, the word thick in her mouth.

She closed her eyes.

It didn't matter anyway.

Monsters quite often do very
surprising things.

P.K. Mayberry's Complete Guide to
Monsters of the Northern Hemisphere

Mary-Kate was coughing when she woke. She was coughing in a way she'd never coughed before, as though she could cough up the whole inside of herself. It was an exhausting business. Tears streamed from her eyes. Through these tears several blurred faces appeared and disappeared above her. A bushy red beard and bald head. Black spiky hair and pink glasses. And someone who looked very much like …

'Lord Woolington,' she spluttered.

'It's all right, Mary-Kate. Sit up,' Terry was saying, patting her gently on the back. 'Your mother's coming across the field right now.'

Mary-Kate looked down at her body and saw her navy-blue dress was coated in slime. Her black stockings unrecognisable. Her red sparkly shoes charred.

'Where's Arabella?' she coughed.

'She's right beside you,' said Terry.

They were in the field before Round Hill and Arabella was sitting near her, supported by her father. He was dabbing at his daughter's nose and eyes with the lucky handkerchief.

'I'm so sorry, so very sorry,' he was muttering. 'I stopped the gas as soon as I learned you were both down there.'

Arabella was gazing up at her father, her face very pale. Pickles was also nearby, munching on grass.

'It's all right Papa,' Arabella said groggily. 'The wyrm helped us out. Can you believe it, Mary-Kate?'

'Pardon?' gasped Mary-Kate.

'It's true,' said Terry, a look of awe in his eyes. 'We saw the wyrm bring you out, didn't we, Ms Honey? It had you both on its back. It dropped you on the ground, turned around and went back in.'

'But the gas!' cried Mary-Kate, which made her cough even more.

Yolanda Honey's face reappeared. She patted

Mary-Kate on the back this time.

'It's all right, Mary-Kate,' she said. 'I got there in the nick of time. He'd only just started to pump it in!'

The librarian glared at Lord Woolington before continuing.

'It was enough gas to put you two poor things to sleep, but not a creature that size. Thankfully, Pickles brought the note to me at the library when I was just preparing to leave and chain myself in the square. I'd finally worked up the courage, you see.'

'Pickles!' cried Mary-Kate and Arabella in unison. It brought on a fresh bout of coughing for both of them. They were encouraged to lay back onto the ground. Mary-Kate stared into the sky that had cleared to blue and took great gulps of the fresh air. Pickles! Could she still be dreaming?

'Mary-Kate!' Professor Martin was beside her. 'Are you hurt?'

'Prof!' wheezed Mary-Kate. It felt so good to have her mother beside her. 'It was real. We helped it and it helped us back.'

'I'm very proud of you, Mary-Kate,' said Professor Martin. 'And you too, Arabella.'

'And Pickles was a hero too,' said Arabella, proudly.

'Yes, he was waiting right outside the library door!' said Yolanda, continuing her story. 'I saw the note in his bridle and read it out. I dropped the chain right there and rushed to the square to find your mother, Mary-Kate. I found Lord Woolington instead pumping sleeping gas down into the subterranean tunnel.'

Lord Woolington began helping Arabella to her feet. His cheeks were very red.

'I never would have if I'd had any idea you girls would be down there,' he said. 'I promise. Arabella! I was so scared for you.'

Mary-Kate saw his hands were trembling as he took Arabella by the shoulders.

'The earth tremors had begun by then,' said Terry.

'That must have been the wyrm turning around,' said Mary-Kate.

Terry nodded. 'I was serving lunch to the Professor and her colleagues. Then there was a such a commotion. The ground was shaking. Ms Honey was yelling. Tyres were screeching. Of course I wanted to hide, but this time, well, the Professor insisted I get up, and I'm so glad that she did. We raced to the square just in time to see Lord Woolington rushing off in his car on the way to Round Hill.'

'Terry and I grabbed the first form of transport we could find,' said the librarian, smiling.

Mary-Kate looked puzzled until Yolanda nodded at Pickles.

'That pony can really gallop,' said Terry.

'Pickles really is a hero!' shouted Arabella. Pickles raised his head from where he was chomping grass and looked most disinterested.

'We arrived just in time,' started Yolanda.

'To see the wyrm emerge and drop you on the ground,' added Terry.

'Did you see it, Papa?' asked Arabella, gazing up at Lord Woolington.

Lord Woolington glanced at the others. He fidgeted with his tie and raked a hand through his hair. There were others arriving now. Mr Blair; Moira, her arm in a cast; Graham looking sheepish; and down below, another car arriving with the team of archaeologists from London, all of them racing up the hill. In the distance, across the fields, other villagers were approaching; Mrs Beattie was being pushed in her wheelchair.

'Come, Arabella,' Lord Woolington said. 'We must go home.'

'It saved us, Papa. The wyrm saved us. It brought us out on its back.'

'Now, now, Arabella, we know there's no such thing as the wyrm,' Lord Woolington said, glancing around at the others again.

'Why were you pumping gas down that hole then?' asked Yolanda.

'I – I—' stammered Lord Woolington. His shoulders slumped.

'We heard you,' said Mary-Kate. She took the phone from her pocket, swiped the voice memo app open. She was still recording! She'd never even had a chance to stop it. They might have no photo, but they had Lord Woolington's words. She moved her finger backwards along the recording line.

'*Go and get some lunch, Graham. Pretend you never saw me here. I've got to do what's right for the village of Woolington Well and the Woolington name.*'

Those words were loud in the silence on the hill.

'I was only doing what I thought was right,' said Lord Woolington. 'I was scared. Scared of what would become of our village. How could it ever prosper if all it was known for was the wyrm? I wanted to change that. I was scared of what it might do to us. I saw it when I was a child, you know. I've always been … scared of the wyrm.'

Arabella nodded solemnly. She hugged her father.

'Papa,' she said. Her face was coated with slime, her blonde hair turned brown. 'I know you think that was the best thing to do. It's all you've been thinking about for years. Building the shopping centre so Woolington isn't known for the wyrm. But I didn't know you were scared.'

Lord Woolington's bottom lip quivered. He looked at the sky.

'The wyrm doesn't hurt anyone,' she continued. 'Mary-Kate found out it never ate any children and she formed a theory. It only gets angry when there's noise and vibrations, and too much light in its tunnel. It can't even see. Usually, it never bothers anyone. It deserves to be here just as much as any of us.'

'I second that!' said Yolanda.

'Hear, hear!' cried Moira.

'I don't want you to go ahead with the shopping centre, Papa. Please put the well back together,' said Arabella. She had her hands on her hips.

Mary-Kate stood up too, with the help of Professor Martin.

'I know that all those hundreds of years ago the people blamed the Woolingtons, but now it's different,' she said. 'If my theory is correct then it doesn't really want to harm anyone. In fact, more than anything, *it* is scared. As scared as all of us are. It is just as scared as you!'

She looked at Terry, who had been so brave. Yolanda, standing tiny and fierce in the sunlight. Mrs Beattie, who had finally made it to the small circle, her carer pushing her. She was beaming.

It was time for Lord Woolington to be brave too.

'Arabella is right,' continued Mary-Kate. 'The wyrm deserves its well. It saved a Woolington today, after all. And it saved me. You could build a museum instead. It could be all about the wyrm. People would come from all over to see that.'

'I would be happy to be involved in setting this up, Lord Woolington,' said Yolanda. 'I could apply for a grant and perhaps you would consider contributing some funds. We could refurbish the Town Hall using a fraction of the money you would be spending on the shopping centre.'

'I could organise tours to Wyrm Hole,' suggested Terry. 'We wouldn't go far in – the wyrm must be left in peace – but just to the entrance. Visitors would love that.'

'I could drive the bus,' said Graham shyly, apparently not sure if his Wyrm Watch Society colleagues would trust him so soon.

'I'd bake wyrm-themed morning teas!' cried Moira, the baker.

Lord Woolington looked around at them all,

tears glistening in his eyes.

'It's the proper thing to do,' said Arabella.

'It's your own special monster,' said Mary-Kate. 'It belongs to Woolington Well and Woolington Well should look after it.'

The Rule of Monsters states
that people who have met one
monster are statistically much
more likely to meet another.

P.K. Mayberry's Complete Guide to
Monsters of the Northern Hemisphere

Mary-Kate lay tucked beneath the covers of her four-poster bed. She wore her blue silk Japanese pyjamas and the star-shaped medal pinned to her chest. Her strawberry-scented notebook was nestled beneath her pillow. Her sparkly red shoes and her slime-ridden clothes had been placed in a plastic bag. After an hour of lying in the bath, all the dirt, slime and grime on her had dissolved.

She had been checked over by a doctor who had driven from Lessington and listened to her lungs before declaring she was fine. The doctor had put ointment on the cuts and bruises and advised her against doing anything that dangerous again. Mary-Kate had politely agreed. She was almost one hundred per cent certain she would never need to do anything like *that* again.

She looked at the medal. She touched the old

magenta, green and blue ribbon.

'Your turn now,' Arabella had said, unpinning it on Round Hill.

'Thank you,' Mary-Kate had replied.

'Will you write to me?'

'Yes, of course.' Mary-Kate had stared at the ground. She always had trouble with endings. Endings gave her stomach nerves. Endings were like cliffs and mountain sides and …

'I can tell you how the museum is going,' said Arabella.

Lord Woolington had agreed to the museum. He had agreed to everything that Arabella had demanded of him, there in the field. He had shaken his head so sadly, as though realising his foolishness, until even Yolanda had patted him on the shoulder. Mary-Kate was certain that Arabella and the members of the Wyrm Watch Society would make the museum a reality.

Mary-Kate's eyes grew heavy, lying there on the bed. A comfortable, calm heavy. Many things made Mary-Kate feel better: the right amount of sparkle, paints in unopened pots and thirty-minute infomercials on steam mops. And now the solving of monster mysteries could be added to the list. *Monster hunting*. That word echoed softly in her head.

There are those that hunt monsters to harm them and there are those that hunt monsters to help them.

She had so many questions. Why had Mrs Beattie said she'd met the Prof before? Was Mary-Kate's mother a monster hunter too? And who were the people that Lord Woolington had mentioned, the ones that were coming to collect the wyrm? Did they harm or help? Her eyelids drooped just thinking these things.

You, Mary-Kate, with your wonderful assistant Arabella, are most definitely the latter.

They were the helpers. Yet, she knew it was even more than saving the wyrm. The village would go back to the way it was. The villagers would return. The little cottages would have flowers in their gardens again. The old oak trees on the green would survive.

'I wish I knew what it means,' Mary-Kate said dreamily, touching the words on the medal. 'I'll need to look it up when we can get somewhere with internet.'

Professor Martin came to stand beside her.

'It's Latin,' she said, smiling down at Mary-Kate. 'This word is courage. This word is knowledge. And this word is kindness.'

'And what about these little letters?'

On the reverse side of the medal there were four very small letters separated by dots: *W. S. M. H.*

'Maybe that is your next mystery to solve.' Professor Martin smiled.

'I'm too tired for any more mysteries,' said Mary-Kate, yawning. 'I hope the wyrm will be okay.'

'It was a fine specimen by the sound of it and I hope it will be okay too.' She kissed Mary-Kate on the forehead. 'You were very, very brave today. You did well for your first time.'

Mary-Kate closed her eyes, overcome with weariness. She couldn't even comprehend the largeness of that day.

Her mother's words – *a fine specimen* – drifted through her mind. That was a strange thing to say. Even stranger, her words *first time*.

Would there be another time? she wondered drowsily as she began to fall asleep.

More monster-hunting adventures would have to wait for another day.

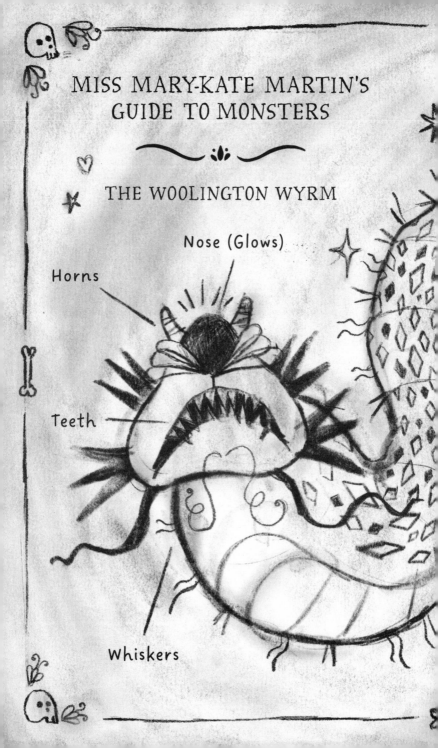

MISS MARY-KATE MARTIN'S GUIDE TO MONSTERS

THE WOOLINGTON WYRM

Nose (Glows)

Horns

Teeth

Whiskers

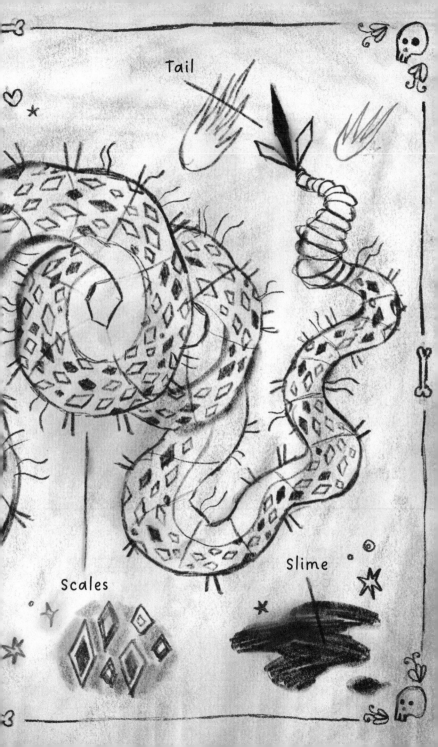

Tail

Scales

Slime

Acknowledgements

There are many wonderful wyrm legends in the British Isles and numerous towns associated with such creatures. The Laidley, the Linton, the Lambton and the Sockburn wyrms are all good examples of such wyrm stories. I used bits and pieces from these ancient tales to construct the Woolington Wyrm in my story.

Thank you to Freda Chiu for bringing the wyrm to life in all his wonderful brown glittery sliminess. I am so grateful for all her delightful illustrations in this book. They make me happy each time I look at them. Thanks also to Hannah Janzen for her book design.

I would like to thank Anna McFarlane and Nicola Santilli at Allen & Unwin. They have helped me, yet again, to expand on a rough first draft in just the right places. Their suggestions are always brilliant and I'm so lucky to have them cheering on my ideas. And very special thanks to Edwina Wyatt and Katrina Nannestad for being first readers.

Finally, thanks to Alice May, who I've dedicated this book to, for always bringing the sunshine.

Mary-Kate's
legendary adventures
continue in . . .

The Trouble with the
Two-headed Hydra

Read an
excerpt from
Book 2!

The monster slid swiftly beneath the surface. Barely a ripple passed above where the ferry rode the gentle waves.

Onboard, passengers dozed on the deck in the sunshine or drank coffees at the bar. Two men argued over a game of cards. An old woman stood up to stretch her legs, holding onto her cane. Three small girls danced to the traditional Greek music playing over the ferry's PA system.

The sun shone brilliantly and the boat skimmed over the calm seas. Down beneath, the monster writhed. Its dark blue scales glimmered.

The captain, in his crisp white shorts and shirt, took the microphone and the PA system crackled. He pointed to the small port in the distance, the hills covered in the houses and hotels.

'Welcome to the isle of Galini,' he said. 'Did you know it means tranquillity?'

No one sensed what lurked below.

The Rule of Monsters states
that people who have met one monster
are statistically much more
likely to meet another.

P.K. Mayberry's Complete Guide to

Monsters of the Northern Hemisphere

Mary-Kate stared at her outfit in the mirror. Brand new sparkly red shoes, blue shorts and a blue and white striped T-shirt. She wondered what she needed to balance the stripes. Her red sparkly backpack had helped, but she needed something else. She sighed and looked through her bow box. A bow was definitely what she needed. A red bow or a blue bow or preferably a navy bow patterned with small white anchors. She knew she owned no such bow, but she looked anyway. She placed the plain navy bow in her long brown hair and sighed again.

She'd tried very hard to create a coordinated seaside theme with her clothes because she knew it would make her feel better. If everything in her suitcase matched, nothing terrible could possibly happen, but she didn't own nearly enough nautical type attire. Professor Martin, Granny and Mary-

Kate only went once a year to Scarborough, but that wasn't really the same as the Greek Islands. Just thinking the words Greek Islands made her stomach begin to churn with butterflies. The *Greek Islands* were far, far away. There was deep ocean and tall mountains in-between with potential for great calamities. Avalanches maybe. Quite possibly volcanoes.

Thinking *volcanoes* made her go straight to her lucky items collection, which was stored neatly on the top shelf of her bookstand. She took her lucky silver packet of chewing gum that now contained the last six pieces of gum her father had left behind before he disappeared on Mount Shishapangma when she was five. She placed it in her shorts pocket. She took her lucky international coin collection in its new jar and placed it in her red sparkly backpack. She touched the old jar, which now contained Woolington Wyrm slime. It was brown and glittered slightly. Even though she shuddered, a strange thrill of excitement also coursed through her and her breath caught in her throat.

'La-la-la,' she said aloud so she would stop thinking about that adventure and continued to sift through her collection. She would definitely need her lucky Big Ben-shaped novelty torch, she decided, and she was almost certain she should take the miniature music box that played Swan Lake. She quickly placed these items into her backpack, followed by her lucky protractor and compass set. She took a deep breath, picked up her lucky world globe stress ball and squished it hard, then added it to the pile. She placed her strawberry-scented notebook and her glitter pens on top.

Finally, she opened the top dresser drawer and retrieved something that she'd only recently acquired. It was a star-shaped medal attached to an old striped ribbon. The colours were magenta, blue and green. She slipped it into her pocket beside the chewing gum.

'Just in case,' she murmured to herself.

'Mary-Kate,' called her mother, Professor Martin.

'Can you bring your suitcase to the front door? The driver will be here in a minute. And then run upstairs to say goodbye to Granny. Don't forget to pack your bathers.'

'Okay,' called Mary-Kate, glancing at her hideously patterned bathers that lay draped over the chair. Mary-Kate was a good swimmer, but her bathers were green and decorated with cats in boats. Her granny had bought them for her.

'Patterns are good,' her granny sometimes said when she came downstairs in a floral skirt and a striped shirt and an emerald-green overcoat. She liked to smile at Mary-Kate to see if she'd disagree. Mary-Kate loved her granny, even with clashing patterns, but sometimes her outfits were so brightly mismatched that Mary-Kate had to look away and hope that a disaster wouldn't happen. It wasn't just mismatched clothes that set off these thoughts of disaster though, many things could.

For instance:

✴ Brown colouring-in pencils

* Beginnings and endings
* Facing backwards on trains
* Saying the wrong thing during small talk
* Or sudden changes.

And there had been a rather large sudden change in the Martin household since the phone rang late last night. Professor Martin had been summoned to an important find in an archaeological dig on a remote Greek Island. She'd come into the sitting room where Granny and Mary-Kate had been watching the shopping channel and informed Mary-Kate that she'd be coming on the trip as well.

'Me?' Mary-Kate had gasped. She hadn't long returned from Woolington Well with the Professor and the adventure she'd had there still filled her head with a mix of dread, confusion and strange fluttery excitement.

'Oh, the Greek Islands are simply wonderful. You'll love it, Mary-Kate,' cried Granny, popping another Turkish delight in her mouth. 'What's the find, dear?'

'A wonderful tiled floor unearthed in the expansion of a fish processing plant. Shows some type of sea creature, apparently,' said the Professor.

'C-creature,' stammered Mary-Kate. She'd been looking forward to her term holidays from Bartley Towers, time spent with Granny and the soothing sounds of the shopping channel.

'It's made of tile, darling, it should be safe.' Granny smiled. 'Oh, how wonderful, a fabulous adventure on a Greek Island. If only I hadn't had that small accident on my bus tour to Birmingham, I'd have come along too.'

Granny had sprained her ankle and was confined to her chair or a bed for a week.

'Creature,' whispered Mary-Kate now. She glanced at the Woolington Wyrm slime in the jar on her lucky things shelf. In Woolington Well she'd met Lady Arabella Woolington and together they'd crawled through muddy tunnels and met a giant fire-breathing wyrm. They'd solved a mystery and helped a monster and saved a village. She'd done things that she never, ever would have thought herself capable of.

Mary-Kate purposefully left the hideous bathers where they were and zipped up her suitcase.

Surely nothing like that could EVER happen again ... right?

About the Author

Karen Foxlee is an Australian author who writes for both kids and young adults. She grew up in the Australia outback mining town Mount Isa and still frequently dreams she is walking barefoot along the dry Leichhardt River.

Ophelia and the Marvellous Boy, Karen's first novel for children, was published internationally to much acclaim while her second novel for younger readers, *A Most Magical Girl*, won the Readings Children's Fiction Prize in 2017 and was CBCA short-listed the same year. Her next book was the internationally successful *Lenny's Book of Everything*, which has won multiple awards including the NSW

Premier's Literary Award, the Indies Book Award, the Queensland Literary Award, was a CBCA Honour Book and was nominated for the Carnegie Medal. Her latest novel, *Dragon Skin*, was a CBCA Notable Book and short-listed for the Indie Book Awards.

Karen lives in South East Queensland with her daughter and several animals, including two wicked parrots, who frequently eat parts of her laptop when she isn't looking. Her passions are her daughter, writing, daydreaming, baking, running and swimming in the sea.

About the Illustrator

Freda Chiu is an author and illustrator from Sydney, Australia. As well as illustrating children's books, her work spans comics, editorial and retail graphics.

Outside her art practice, Freda lectures in Illustration at the University of Technology Sydney.

Freda's debut picture book, *A Trip to the Hospital*, was short-listed for the IBBY Australia Ena Noël Award.